Belles Saisons

Belles Saisons

A COLETTE SCRAPBOOK

ASSEMBLED, AND WITH

COMMENTARY, BY

ROBERT PHELPS

Farrar, Straus and Giroux

New York

for Bel Gazou

Copyright © 1978 by Robert Phelps

All rights reserved

Published simultaneously in Canada by McGraw-Hill Ryerson Ltd., Toronto

Printed in the United States of America

Designed by Cynthia Krupat

First edition, 1978

Library of Congress Cataloging in Publication Data

Phelps, Robert.   Belles saisons.   Bibliography

1. Colette, Sidonie Gabrielle, 1873–1954—Iconography.

2. Authors, French—20th century—   Iconography. I. Title.

PQ2605.028Z776   848'.9'1209   [B]   78–6944

CONTENTS

First and always a verbal artist, the author of *La vagabonde, Chéri, Sido, Le pur et l'impur,* and a dozen other books which have become landmarks in European literature, Colette was also a very original human being, an earthbound, androgynous, profoundly French female whose personality so deeply saturated everything she wrote that her life has begun to attract readers as much as her art. It is as though she had a secret which she never revealed directly, which perhaps she herself could never have formulated, yet which we can now recognize in her temperament and personal history.

An eager country girl from Burgundy, she came to Toulouse-Lautrec's Paris at twenty, already married to a literary hack, under whose pen name she ghostwrote a series of autobiographical novels that made her notorious. After a painful divorce, she found her way onto the music-hall stage, lived for several years with another woman, presently married a handsome young newspaper editor, and at forty became a dazzled mother. At the same time, she continued to write novels, short stories, personal essays, plays, memoirs, which she now published under her own name. In her fifties, she was divorced a second time, and was married again, to a man she always referred to as her "best friend." In her sixties, generally acknowledged the finest stylist writing in French, she produced further novels, all short, precise, and dealing exclusively with what Tolstoy called, "for all time, man's most tormenting tragedy—the tragedy of the bedroom." In her seventies, she survived the Nazi occupation of Paris, and went on writing in spite of a crippling arthritis. She died at eighty-one, *en pleine gloire,* as intimately known to three generations of her countrymen as the Tour Eiffel.

Belles Saisons amounts to the sort of scrapbook Colette herself might have kept: photographs, drawings, and marginal anecdotes by friends and confreres. If her life has a secret, its intimation lies somewhere in these pages, implicit perhaps, but pervasive, penetrating, and, however expressed, having something to do with what Shakespeare meant when at the end of his own life he said, "Ripeness is all."

R.P.

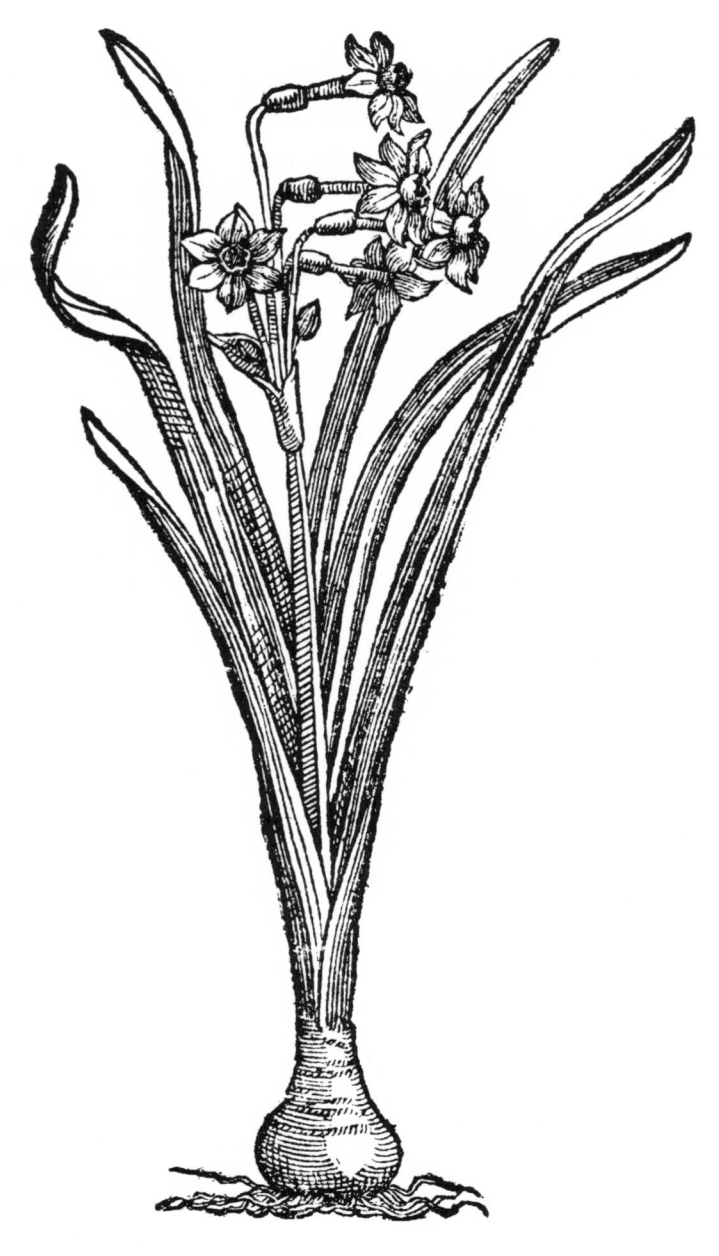

1 9 5 4 – 7 3

En Pays Connu

*Le Père Couturier dit avoir rendu visite
à Matisse et à Colette "qui tous deux
vont au Paradis sans un pli."*

*Father Couturier said he had visited Colette and
Matisse. "Beyond the shadow of a doubt both
of them will go to Heaven."*

JULIEN GREEN, *Journal*

❦ Her cumulative name would have been Sidonie-Gabrielle Colette Willy Gauthiers-Villars de Jouvenel des Ursins Goudeket. But at eighty-one and a half years of age she was known to three generations of readers, worldwide, by her patronymic alone: Colette.

On the Tuesday evening of August 3, 1954, she lay on her bed—her raft, as she called it—in a tiny room with red silk walls and a single casement window overlooking the deserted gardens of the Palais-Royal, in the very heart of Paris. The weather was sultry, the sky overcast. She had been sleeping for some time, and what were to become her last recorded words had been uttered a few hours earlier. Indicating a flight of swallows that swooped and crisscrossed in the sky over the garden, she had murmured, "Ah, look! Look!"

Now the only sound was her breathing. Then suddenly there was silence. It was a little past eight-thirty, and "by a movement of infinite grace, her head slipped slowly to one side."

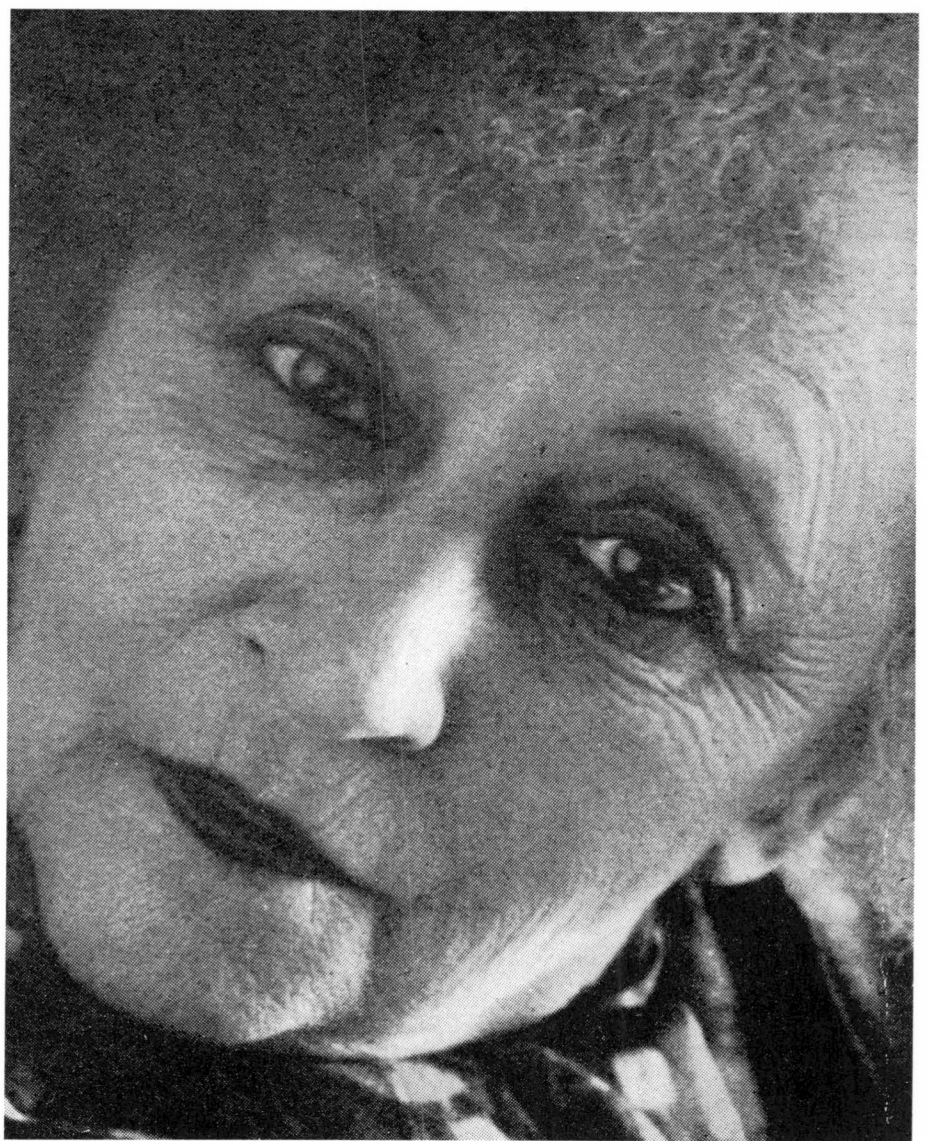

❧ There was a state funeral, with a tricolor-draped catafalque, in the Cour d'Honneur of the Palais-Royal, and with masses of flowers from anonymous readers as well as illustrious names: red roses from Queen Elisabeth of Belgium, pink lilies from the Association of Music-Halls and Circuses, dahlias from Saint-Sauveur-en-Puisaye, Colette's Burgundy birthplace. There was also a brief scandal. Cardinal Feltin, Archbishop of Paris, saw fit to admonish Colette posthumously by forbidding the presence of a priest at her funeral. His Eminence, in turn, was admonished by British novelist Graham Greene in *Le Figaro Littéraire* for August 7:

"Today, by your decision, no priest offered public prayers at Colette's funeral. We all know your reasons. But would they have been brought forward if Colette had been less famous? Forget the great writer and think only of an old woman of eighty who, at a time when Your Eminence had not yet been ordained, made an unhappy marriage through no fault of her own (unless innocence is a fault) and later broke the Church's law by a second and then a third civil marriage. Are two civil marriages so unforgivable? The lives of some of our saints provide worse examples . . . Of course, upon reflection, Catholics may consider that the voice of an Archbishop is not necessarily the voice of the Church."

❧ Pauline Tissandier, Colette de Jouvenel, and Maurice Goudeket, respectively Colette's caretaker, daughter, and *"meilleur ami."*

From the Palais-Royal, the services moved on to a plot in the Père-Lachaise Cemetery near the intersection of the avenue Principale and the avenue Circulaire. There, as Jean Cocteau (himself unable to attend because of a heart attack) observed, "it was less a matter of funeral ceremonies than of gardeners at work, transplanting."

❦ Colette, in a charcoal drawing made about 1947 by Jean Cocteau. "In the last fifteen years of Colette's life, Jean was our dearest friend" (Goudeket). And it was with the authority of this intimacy that Cocteau wrote one of the most candid evaluations of Colette's personality published so far: "We shall never sufficiently cleanse Madame Colette of the false nicety with which her legend continues to muffle her . . . Don't take her for just a nice little old lady. Her velvet paw could show its claws very fast. And when she scratched, she left a gash."

A holograph page from one of Colette's last manuscripts, *"Ces dames anciennes,"* published posthumously in *Belles saisons* in 1955. "How the sight of our admirable Colette's manuscripts have comforted me each time I've seen them. I remember a page in which only a single sentence—one of miraculous ease—had escaped a veritable massacre" (Francis Poulenc).

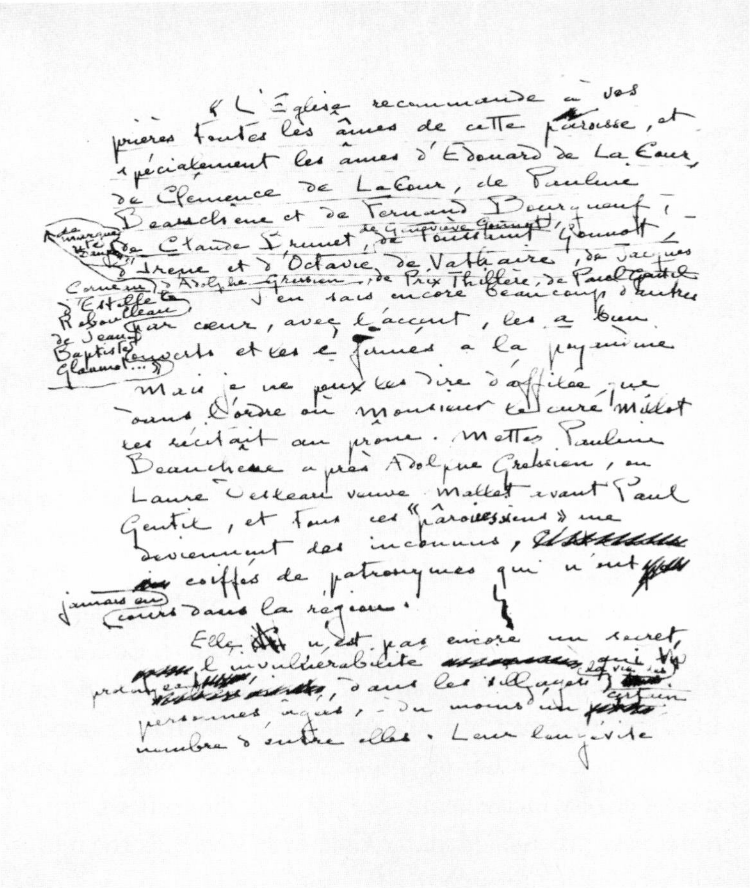

❧ Colette once expressed bemused dismay at the idea that she might be expected to leave "a sort of secret Goncourt Journal" for posthumous publication. "But I've already scraped my drawers of all the material I had. And besides, my life has not been so rich in 'Parisian' adventures."

All the same, the first two decades following her death produced three volumes of stories and memoirs and five of wonderfully live and savory letters. In addition, there were stage adaptations, films, anthologies, and translations. Honors continued to accumulate as well. As of March 1966, it was possible to ask a Paris taxi driver to take you to the Place Colette, on the rue Saint-Honoré, adjoining the Place du Palais-Royal. In Saint-Sauveur, the rue de l'Hospice was changed to the rue Colette. Commemorative plaques adorned both the garden and the street sides of 9, rue de Beaujolais. Then in 1973, the centenary year, the Bibliothèque Nationale organized an extensive exhibition of manuscripts, photographs, rare books, and memorabilia, the catalogue of which remains not only a choice collector's item but, thanks to the collaboration of Madame Colette de Jouvenel, the most comprehensive and satisfying approach to a biography of her mother we yet have.

BIBLIOTHÈQVE NATIONALE

58, rue de Richelieu, Paris 2ᵉ

MAI-SEPTEMBRE 1973

COLETTE

exposition ouverte tous les jours,
dimanches et mardis compris, de 11 heures à 18 heures.

1 8 7 3 – 9 3

Sido

Puissé-je n'oublier jamais que je suis la fille d'une telle femme qui penchait, tremblante, toutes ses rides éblouies entre les sabres d'une cactus sur une promesse de fleur, une telle femme qui ne cessa elle-même d'éclore, infatigablement, pendant trois quarts de siècle.

May I never forget that I am the daughter of a woman who bent, trembling, her lined face dazzled, over the promising bloom of a spear-leafed cactus flower, a woman who never stopped flowering herself, indefatigably, for three quarters of a century.

COLETTE, *La naissance du jour*

Eugène Landoy, Colette's maternal grandfather. "A colored man—a quadroon, I believe," and known in the family as the "Gorilla." Studying his daguerreotype portrait, his daughter Sido conceded that he was "ugly, yes, but well built, and the women hung on him in spite of his violet fingernails."

Adèle-Sophie Landoy, nee Châtenay, Colette's maternal grandmother. "She died young, and twenty times betrayed by her husband. That's all I've ever known about her: in other words, the essentials" (Colette).

Adèle-Eugénie-Sidonie Landoy, Colette's mother, known as "Sido," was born in Paris on August 13, 1835. After her own mother's early death, she lived in Brussels with her brothers, who were journalists and in whose cultivated milieu she acquired her taste for books and her very unprovincial freedom of mind. She was first married in 1857 to a moody, alcoholic man named Jules Robineau-Duclos. His death in 1865 left her with two children and substantial property in Saint-Sauveur-en-Puisaye, a village about one hundred miles southeast of Paris. The same year she was remarried to the man who came to be known as "Le Capitaine."

Jean-Joseph Colette, Colette's paternal grand-father. A pensioned army captain of Italian stock, he had received the Légion d'Honneur and lived in Toulon. Sido referred to him ambiguously as the "man with the knife."

Marie-Thérèse Colette, née Funel, Colette's paternal grandmother, whom she remembered chiefly as *"pas commode,"* not easy to please.

Jules-Joseph Colette, Colette's father, was born in Toulon on September 26, 1829. Trained at the military academy at Saint-Cyr, he served as a captain in the Zouaves, an Algerian light-infantry unit of French soldiers in colorful uniforms. In 1859, he lost his left leg in the battle of Marignano, and was later appointed tax collector at Saint-Sauveur, where he met Sido. "A poet and a townsman," romantic and book-loving, he dreamed all his life of becoming a writer. But his true vocation remained his love for his wife.

Juliette Robineau-Duclos, Colette's elder half sister, *"ma soeur aux longs cheveux."* Born in 1860, she had a somber, estranged childhood. Her marriage, when Colette was twelve, precipitated a bitter legal battle over her inheritance. As her stepfather, the Captain, was unable to account for all of it, the Colette house and furnishings at Saint-Sauveur were sold at public auction in 1890. Juliette had a daughter, but her marriage appears to have been unhappy, and she died a suicide in 1908.

Achille Robineau-Duclos, Colette's elder "half brother by blood, but entire brother by heart, choice, and resemblance." Born in 1863, and quite probably the son of the Captain rather than of his legal father, he studied medicine in Paris and settled in a small town called Châtillon-Coligny, where he worked as a country doctor until his early death, on the last day of 1913.

Leopold Colette, called the "sylph," was born in 1868. A gifted pianist, with an inexhaustible memory bank of his Saint-Sauveur childhood, he lived a quiet bachelor's life as a notary, and died early in 1940, a few months before the Fall of France.

Sidonie-Gabrielle Colette, the youngest of the "savages" in Sido's household, was born "painfully, on January 28, 1873, in a room which it was never possible to keep adequately warm. During my mother's labor, which lasted forty-eight hours, the servants lost their heads, forgetting to add logs to the fireplace, and when I finally emerged, I was so blue and mute that no one thought it worthwhile to bother with me."

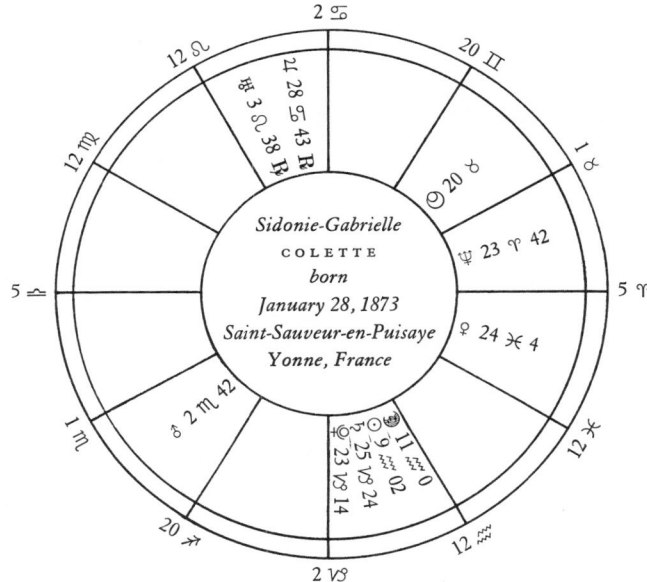

🌷 Colette's natal horoscope, as interpreted by a popular astrologer of the thirties named Marie Louise Sondaz: "A conjunction of Mercury and Saturn . . . in the fourth house . . . gives literary genius, and the fourth house, which is that of the mother, reveals the writer's inspiration: childhood, the mother, vegetable and floral life, early sensations and observations . . . In the order of stars' precedence, Colette is Venus–Moon–Mars ruled: hence the half-feminine, half-masculine nature of this powerful personality." In his *Miroir d'astrologie,* the poet Max Jacob cited Colette in a list of notable Aquarians, adding: "A horror of beaten paths. Very solitary, although loving life, movement, agitation. The Aquarian woman is ambiguous and paradoxical, full of delicacy and incoherence, rebellious on every level. Hers is a cerebral nature which lets itself be guided entirely by the feelings, in the margin of all conformities. Very lofty ideals, in spite of her disorderly existence and her romanticism."

Edition Bergery. Saint-Sauveur

❦ Colette's birthplace: *La maison de Claudine,* in the heart of Basse-Bourgogne. "A large house, solemn, somewhat forbidding . . . a house that smiled only on its garden side. The back, invisible to passers-by, was gilded in sunlight, swathed in a mantle of wistaria."

❦ Colette and her brother Leo in the garden: ". . . and begonia too heavy for the trellis of worn ironwork, which sagged in the middle like a hammock and provided shade for the little flagged terrace and the threshold of the sitting room."

❦ Sido at forty-five, about 1880. "On the first of May, with my comrades of the catechism class, I laid lilac, camomile, and roses before the altar of the Virgin, and came home full of pride to show my 'blessed posy.' My mother laughed her irreverent laugh and . . . said: 'Do you suppose it wasn't blessed before?' "

❦ Colette at five (1878),
at eleven (1884), and
at fifteen (1888)

❧ On the doorstep of young Dr. Achille Robineau-Duclos's house in Châtillon-Coligny, where the Colette family took refuge after the loss of their Saint-Sauveur home. *Clockwise:* the Captain, Sido, Achille, Colette, Leo.

❧ Colette in the spring of 1893, on the brink of marriage

❧ Colette at twenty, reading in the garden at Châtillon-Coligny, perhaps a volume of the Houssiaux edition of Balzac, the "religion of my adolescence, the guide of my earliest education."

❧ The Captain and Sido, playing dominoes. "What a pity," Sido once wrote, "he should have loved me so much! It was his love for me that destroyed, one after another, all those splendid abilities he had for literature and the sciences. He preferred to think only of me, to torment himself for me, and that was what I found inexcusable. So great a love! What frivolity!"

❦ Henri Gauthiers-Villars, at twenty, in his army uniform. Known professionally as Willy (pronounced in the English manner: not Vee-lee, but plain Will-y), he was born in 1859, the son of one of the leading publishers of scientific books in France. When he met Colette, he was in his thirties, with a volume of sonnets as well as a book about Mark Twain behind him. But even at this early stage, his literary production was bipartite and almost entirely ghost-written. On the one hand, there was pulp fiction of a slick, cynical, Naughty Nineties caste: *Une passade, Un vilain monsieur, Maîtresse d'esthètes,* etc.; and on the other, a body of music criticism (collected in ten volumes) that was zestful, courageous, and briskly *à la page:* Willy was among the earliest defenders of Debussy, Ravel, Fauré, and the Russian Five.

❦ The courtship. Gathered in the sitting room: Willy, Colette, Sido, and the Captain. "The infatuation of a girl in love is neither as constant nor as blind as she tries to believe. But her pride keeps her brave and self-contained, even in the moments when she will utter the inevitable and sincere great cry of awakening and fear. That cry had not risen to my lips, for two long years of engagement had settled my fate without altering anything in my life. After becoming my fiancé, the family friend came to see us rather infrequently, bringing books, magazines, sweets, and then leaving."

❦ May 15, 1893. Colette, in her white muslin dress, walks through the street on the Captain's arm. Fifty years later, in the darkest time of the Occupation, she wrote a brief, unsentimental account of that day: "A quiet and modest wedding . . . No Mass, merely a benediction in the afternoon at four o'clock. At five, Sido took a short rest, very prim in her faille silk dress with jet trimmings. She was flushed, as always when she felt unhappy and was trying to conceal it . . . As for the rest, I can only say that I looked quite nice and was rather pale."

1 8 9 3 – 1 9 0 6

Mes Apprentissages

Rien d'ailleurs ne rassure autant qu'un masque.

There is nothing that gives more assurance than a mask.

COLETTE, *Mes apprentissages*

❧ Colette and Willy on their honeymoon. "My life as a woman began with this buccaneer, a serious match for a country girl. Before him, my entire life—except for my parents' bankruptcy and the furniture sold at public auction—had been a bed of roses. But what would I have done with an everlasting bed of roses?"

❧ Colette at twenty-one with Willy's family. At left, her father-in-law, publisher Albert Gauthier-Villars; at extreme right, her mother-in-law; and standing, Willy himself. "In all my life, before my marriage, I had never lived 'in someone else's house,' and it took me a long time to relax the constraint which prevented me, not from loving the in-laws who welcomed me, but from letting myself enjoy the simple pleasure of revealing myself as I was."

The newlyweds settled in the Left Bank's 6th arrondissement, in a third-floor apartment at 28, rue Jacob, a tiny street two blocks long where Racine had lived in 1656 and Stendhal in 1810, and where Wagner had finished *The Flying Dutchman* in 1842. As music critic for the *Echo de Paris,* Willy had access to the most fashionable salons devoted to the arts, and very soon Colette had met and been admired by Anatole France, Léon Daudet, Marcel Proust, and Paul Valéry, as well as César Franck, Gabriel Fauré, Vincent d'Indy, Ravel, and Debussy. What is possibly the first reference to her name in French literature appears in an entry for November 6, 1894, in the *Journal* of Jules Renard: at the opening night of Maurice Maeterlinck's production of *'Tis Pity She's a Whore,* she was noticed for her laugh and "a braid of hair long enough to let the bucket down a well with."

But the rue Jacob apartment had no sun, little light, less air, and then one day Colette discovered her husband's chronic infidelity. "Dressed in my handsome, 125-franc coat, my serpent of hair bound with a new ribbon, I took a cab to the rue Bochart-de-Saron and rang the bell of a minute, mezzanine-floor flat. Anonymous letters often tell the truth. There, in fact, were M. Willy and Mlle Charlotte Kinceler, not in bed but sitting in front of—yes!—an open account book. M. Willy was holding the pencil . . . I listened to the pulse beating in my tonsils, and the two lovers stared, astounded, at the pale young provincial . . . What could I say? A dark little woman was watching me, a pair of scissors grasped tightly in her hand; a word, a movement, and she would have flown at my face . . . M. Willy sat mopping his brow."

Shortly after this incident, Colette began to languish. There was no satisfactory medical diagnosis, but Sido came to nurse her (from this date addressing her son-in-law as Monsieur Willy), and after two months she revived, having gotten over "the worst thing in a woman's life, her first man, the only one you die of."

❧ Marcel Schwob, from a caricature by Sacha Guitry which Colette called "the only portrait of Schwob which looked like Schwob." The son of a cultivated family of doctors and rabbis, Marcel Schwob (1867–1905) was one of Colette's earliest and dearest Parisian friends, and an all-around *homme de lettres.* As a scholar, he published studies of fifteenth-century French argot; as a translator, he brought *Moll Flanders* into French; as a playwright, he adapted *Hamlet* for Sarah Bernhardt; as a novelist, he wrote *Le livre de Monelle,* the story of a prostitute who died miserably of tuberculosis. It was as an editor of the weekly *Echo de Paris,* for which Willy wrote the music criticism, that he met twenty-year-old Colette. During her illness of 1894, he would climb three floors at the rue Jacob daily and read his translations of Mark Twain and Dickens to distract her. "I treated him as though he belonged to me," she said, and Schwob, in turn, "loved Colette tenderly, teased her cruelly, and admired her without reserve" (Moreno).

❧ "It seems to me, in the last analysis, that Colette's greatest friend was Marguerite Moreno" (Goudeket). Born in Paris in 1871, she was already associated with the Comédie Française when Colette met her at a luncheon party about "1894—or '95." "I had neither eyes nor ears for anyone but this tall young woman, her wit, her easy and sparkling delivery, the timbre of her voice which rejoiced the ear . . . the warm look in her unwavering, lively eyes that scorned any coquettish appeal. Everything about her enchanted the bewildered little country girl I was at the time." Moreno's theatrical career was long and various, and with the advent of sound films, she became one of the busiest and most popular character actresses in France. Colette's letters to her incarnate half a century of love, intimacy, tenderness, and candor.

[40] It was to Moreno, in 1931, that Colette wrote: "You must tell me what you think of something I'm writing just now on 'unisexuals'—ghastly word! Obviously, one could treat the whole subject in one sentence: There *are* no unisexuals."

🌺 Paul Masson, an ex-colonial magistrate of Chandernagore, India, and Colette's "other friend and daily visitor" during her illness. "Thanks to him, I came to value a little more highly what there was in me that was unusual, attractive, desolate, secret." At the time he was close to the Willy ménage, he was on the staff of the Bibliothèque Nationale, into whose catalogue of books he cynically inserted imaginary titles. "But why," Colette asked, "if the books don't exist?" "Ah!" replied Masson, "I can't do everything." A masterful maker of puns and a lover of jokes, he wrote under the pseudonym Lemice-Térieux. But his surest place in literature will be secured by Colette's tartly affectionate portraits of him: one, under the name of Masseau, in *L'entrave;* and the other, undisguised, in *Mes apprentissages.* "His death was a classic example of a humorist's end: standing on the banks of the Rhine, he pressed a pad soaked in ether to his face until his legs gave way. He fell and was drowned in a foot of water."

🌺 Pierre Louÿs (1870–1925), Symbolist poet and novelist (*Aphrodite*), friend of Gide and Valéry, was best known in the Belle-Epoque for his *Chansons de Bilitis, traduites du grec par Pierre Louÿs,* a collection of prose poems of love supposedly written by a contemporary of Sappho. They had a substantial influence on Colette's own early prose (*Les vrilles de la vigne,* in particular), and a number were set to music by Debussy. Louÿs moved in Willy's circles and was the author of *Dialogue au soleil couchant,* in which, one fine summer afternoon on the lawn of Natalie Clifford Barney's house in Neuilly, Colette made her amateur debut as a mime.

❧ Maurice Ravel (1875–1937), whom Colette first encountered in the exclusively musical salon of Madame de Saint-Marceaux, where Debussy and Chabrier, d'Indy and Fauré, all gathered on Wednesday evenings to talk shop and play four-handed duets. "He was young, not yet at the age which prefers simplicity, with side whiskers—yes!—and a voluminous crop of hair which exaggerated the contrast between his sizable head and his slight body. He loved showy ties and ruffled shirts. At the same time that he sought attention, he feared criticism, and that of Henri Gauthiers-Villars was cruel to him. Perhaps, too, he was secretly timid, for he maintained a remote manner and spoke in a dry tone of voice."

Just before the First World War, the Paris Opéra proposed that Colette and Ravel collaborate on an opera, and Colette produced a libretto which "I thoughtlessly called *Divertissement pour ma fille* until the day Ravel said to me in an icy tone, 'I have no daughter . . .'" Ravel's radiant score was finished in 1925, but by then there was a new title: *L'enfant et les sortilèges.*

❧ Claude Debussy (1862–1918), photographed by Pierre Louÿs, 1894. It was in "the sonorous, lightly feverish warmth" of the same salon that Colette once watched and listened to Debussy trying to reconstruct the precise orchestration of Rimsky-Korsakov's *Scheherazade:* "Lips pursed, then miaowing as he went on to imitate the violins, he panted on, torn apart by all the different timbres vying for places in his memory. With the poker clenched firmly in one hand, he hammered on the rosewood of the piano. With the other he made a zzzzzzzzzzing! sound against the windowpane . . . Then he stood up, using his voice, his arms, and his feet all at once, while two black spirals of hair danced on his forehead. His faun's laugh rang out in reply, not to our laughter, but to some inner soliciting, and I engraved at that moment in my memory the image of our great master of French music in the act of inventing, before our very eyes, the jazz band."

✿ Colette with flowers in her braids.

It was in 1895, two years after her marriage, that Colette wrote the original version of what was to become *Claudine à l'école*. She and Willy had paid a brief visit to Saint-Sauveur, in fact had even stayed overnight in the local schoolhouse, and presently "Willy said to me: 'You ought to put down what you remember of your grade-school days. Don't be afraid of the spicy details. I might be able to do something with it . . . Funds are low.'

"Having found a number of copybooks similar to those I had used at school, I set to work . . . With complete indifference, perched at one corner of the desk, the window behind me, one shoulder hunched and my knees crossed, I wrote.

"When I finished, I gave my husband a manuscript that was closely written and kept within the margins. He read it through and said: 'I was wrong. It's no use at all.' Relieved, I returned to the divan, to my cat, my books, to my new friends, to the life I tried to make pleasant."

✿ Colette with her braids *en chignon.*

Almost five years later, Willy began to clean out his desk. This "odious piece of furniture, hideous in its red baize cover and sham ebony paint, was turned out, the whitewood drawers disgorging a mass of papers, and there came to light the forgotten set of copybooks I had so industriously blackened.

" 'Hello!' said M. Willy. 'I thought I had thrown these away.'

"He opened one and turned the pages: 'It's rather nice . . .'

"He opened a second, then a third, a fourth.

" 'My God!' he muttered. 'I am the bloodiest fool.'

"He swept up the scattered copybooks just as they were, grabbed his flat-brimmed top hat and bolted to his publisher's. And that is how I became a writer."

🌷 Colette with her braids *en macaron*.
"At first, I was conscious only of the boredom of having to set to work again
under pressing and precise directions. 'Couldn't you add a little spice to these
—er—childish affairs?' M. Willy said to me. 'A tender and overintimate affec-
tion, for instance, between Claudine and one of her girl friends . . . And
dialect, lots of dialect. And rather more playfulness . . . Do you see what I
mean?' I saw what he meant, I saw quite well . . . But young women who
write seldom have much sense of moderation . . . And there is nothing that
gives more assurance than a mask."

❧ The original cover of *Claudine à l'école,* published in March 1900, and destined to become a landmark in French literature. On neither the title page nor the copyright page, nor anywhere else, was there any hint that the book was a collaboration. "The origin and anonymity of *Claudine* seemed a rather indelicate joke," Colette wrote some thirty-five years later. "I roared with laughter at the cover: a little girl, disguised as a peasant, sits with an open book on her knee, writing. On her stockinged feet she wears yellow, comic-opera clogs . . . and her curls tumble over her rough, hooded red cloak."

By May, the book had sold 40,000 copies, a phenomenal figure at the time. It was the year of the Paris Exposition, Sarah Bernhardt in *L'Aiglon,* and a saucy little girl called Claudine. But there were serious readers, too. In the prestigious *Mercure de France,* the novelist Rachilde called the book a masterpiece, adding, however, that it promised its author martyrdom as well as fame, since "there will never be enough stones and crowns of thorns to hurl at him."

❦ Caricature of Willy by Rip.

In a letter to Rachilde, Willy gave his version of the unacknowledged collaboration: "I used Colette's notes, and above all her conversations . . . But what would really amuse you would be to see the notes themselves, which, I assure you, I had to feminize and tame down . . . In their original form, before I sweetened them up, they had the spontaneity and coarseness of a tomboy." Toward the end of his life, Willy characterized his role as that of "a marveling professor, who nevertheless insisted on revising his pupil's copy."

Willy, author of the *Claudines.* In all, there were four *Claudine* books: *Claudine à l'école, Claudine à Paris, Claudine en ménage,* and *Claudine s'en va,* published annually from 1900 to 1903, as well as two additional books about another nubile but raffish girl, *Minne* and *Les égarements de Minne.* The last, Colette herself later refashioned into a single novel called *L'ingénue libertine,* and in another novel, wholly her own and published in 1907, *La retraite sentimentale,* she borrowed Claudine as a minor character.

Meantime, Willy enjoyed an extraordinary notoriety in the French-reading world. "As far as I can see," wrote Sacha Guitry in 1904, "only God and perhaps Alfred Dreyfus are more famous than Willy these days."

❧ Colette in 1900.

The original manuscript books of *Claudine à l'école* were destroyed on Willy's orders, so the precise nature of the collaboration will never be determined. However, in her own letter thanking Rachilde for the *Mercure de France* review, Colette seemed to endorse Willy's version. "I had this huge wad of notes in diary form, but I would never have dared believe it readable. Thanks to Belle-Doucette [Willy], who pruned and moderated my crudities, *Claudine* became acceptable." Nor did she ever directly contradict herself, not even when, half a century later, the first *Claudine* and its sequels were published in her *Oeuvres complètes,* for the first time under her own name only: "Their success was immense, inspiring beauty products, girls' fashions, and the theater. Honest, and above all indifferent, I remained quiet about the truth."

❧ Catulle Mendès (1841–1909). Man of letters, editor, and the most feared drama critic of the day, Mendès was also an intimate confrere of Willy and, in the nineties, the lover of Marguerite Moreno. Colette described him as "voluble and full of beer, blond and rufous like Wagner's Siegfried." It was he who turned to her one day at lunch, when Willy had left the table, and said: "You wrote the *Claudines,* didn't you? That's all right, that's all right! I'm not asking questions, you needn't overdo the bashfulness . . . In—in I don't know how long—in twenty years, in thirty years perhaps, people will find out . . . Oh! it's a big thing! Certainly it's a big thing! But it's a sort of punishment too, a guilt that follows you everywhere, that sticks to your skin, a reward that becomes intolerable."

❧ Jules Renard (1864–1910). Author of *Poil de Carotte, Histoires naturelles,* and a posthumous *Journal* which is one of the least sentimental accounts of the literary vocation ever written. "I cannot like Renard," Colette once confessed. "I have never been able to. He was spiteful, wicked, in fact." For his part, Renard keenly admired the *Claudine* books and in a *Journal* entry of 1905 indicated that their dual authorship was an open secret among the *cognoscenti: "Willy ont beaucoup de talent* . . . Willy *have* lots of talent." Even earlier, in a letter of 1903, he had declared that "Claudine is a delicious creature . . . My son, aged fourteen and living at home, has already read *Madame Bovary* [as] . . . he will read all writers of talent. Thus, he'll soon be reading *Claudine."*

🌱 "You can't get away from it—you've created a type." Catulle Mendès to Colette, circa 1903

🌱 Polaire in *Le friquet*

🌱 Polaire in the title role of *Claudine à Paris*. Marie-Emilie Bouchard (1879–1939), known as Polaire, was a music-hall singer with a legendary 17-inch waistline who made her acting debut in January 1902 as the heroine of *Claudine à Paris,* a play which Willy and two ghost writers had concocted out of the first two books of the *Claudine* series. "What Polaire did with her role is unforgettable," said Colette. The play ran on and off in Paris and the provinces for years. It provoked a number of parodies—*Claudine en vadrouille, Claudine et l'apache,* etc. There was even a Polaire Waltz. In November 1908, Colette herself briefly took over the role with a touring company in Brussels and Lyons.

❦ Polaire, Willy, and Colette.

Willy was nothing if not a public-relations expert. In 1902, along with the play, the third of the novels, *Claudine en ménage,* was published. The plot could not have been more worldly. Claudine's cynical husband encourages his kittenish wife in her crush on a seductive woman named Rézi, who turns out to be his own mistress. By way of exploiting this very "Parisian" triangle, Willy arranged to appear in public with Colette and Polaire dressed as twins, proving, as it were, that truth can be as naughty as fiction. On his orders, Colette cut her hair short (to Sido's dismay: "Your hair was not your own. It was mine, the work of twenty years of care and attention"). She and Polaire were then fitted with identical dresses and Willy escorted them to opening nights and fashionable restaurants. "Naturally, people thought the worst, imputing intimate relations to us. Still, if I had asked Polaire to go to bed with me, she would have refused . . . She loved good-looking young boys, the tougher the better."

Willy ~ Polaire
Toby-chien et Colette au
palais de glace
Jean

🌣 Jean Cocteau, in his early teens but precociously *partout* even then, glimpsed the scandalous trio, along with Colette's bulldog, Toby-Chien, at a rinkside table at the Palais de Glace on the Champs-Elysées: "Polaire! A yellow serpent's flat head balancing the Portuguese oysters of her eyes that twinkled with nacre . . . Willy, his huge mustache and *impériale à la Tartarin,* his eyes sharp under their drooping lids . . . And, beside him, our Colette, a slim Colette, a kind of tiny fox in cycling clothes."

On another occasion that same year, Polaire was introduced to Jules Renard, who impaled her on a page of his *Journal:* "A curious little animal, not pretty, who offers her hand awkwardly, at eye level, as though it were a paw."

❦ Madame Colette Willy, at "thirty or thereabouts." "Ten years of Paris; and, appearances notwithstanding, a most singular state of isolation . . . Together, M. Willy and I aroused considerable curiosity; by myself, I aroused no interest of any kind. I could not have put a name to two hundred faces. Thirty, then, and a most unusual dearth of feminine companions, of feminine complicity and support . . . Not that I disliked women particularly, but I was boyish and at ease in the society of men, and I feared women."

Two views of Colette in her gymnasium in the rue de Courcelles. Natalie Clifford Barney, known as "L'Amazone," and one of the first women to live on candid and unanxious terms with her sapphic nature, became Colette's close friend at this time. There is a brief caricature of her as Miss Flossie in *Claudine s'en va,* and in a later volume of memoirs, Miss Barney herself left a shrewdly affectionate portrait of Colette: "At the beginning of the century, when I saw Colette for the first time, she was no longer the thin, long-braided adolescent cradled in a hammock which a photograph shows us. She was a young woman firmly fixed on solid legs, with the small of her back arching down to a full behind; with manners as frank as her speech, but with cat-like silence in her enigmatic, triangular face; and in her beautiful blue-green eyes a look which did not have to appear seductive in order to seduce."

❧ Spanish dancer and courtesan, "La Belle Otéro" was one of a number of demimondaines who befriended Colette in her Willy years and taught her "many great truths":

"'You look a bit green, my girl,' she once said to me. 'Don't forget that there is always a moment in a man's life, even if he is a miser, when he opens his hand *wide* . . .'

"'The moment of passion?'

"'No. The moment when you twist his wrist.'"

✤ Colette was thirty-one years old when she finally saw a book published under—not quite her own name yet—but a combination of her patronymic and her husband's *nom de plume:* Colette Willy.

Called *Dialogues de bêtes,* it consisted of four short conversations between two of her household pets, Kiki-la-Doucette, an Angora cat, and Toby-Chien, a brindled French bulldog. Sido found them "delicious." Willy himself, in a marginal note on the manuscript, spoke of "adorable little marvels." The book was dedicated to Rachilde (incidentally, the only one of Colette's fifty-some books ever to bear a dedication) and was reissued in 1905 with three additional dialogues and an important preface by the poet Francis Jammes which Colette described as the "Rehabilitation of Colette Willy." Indeed, it did challenge for the first time the legend of a naughty girl who had cut her hair short and wore men's clothes: "Seriously speaking, Madame Willy is a vivid woman who has dared to be natural and who is much closer to a little village bride than to a perverse lady of letters."

✤ In addition to writing the preface, Francis Jammes (1868–1938) sent Colette his photograph, inscribed. Acknowledging it, Colette told him he looked like "a monk in the act of taming a rose."

COLETTE WILLY

—

Dialogues de Bêtes

PARIS
SOCIÉTÉ DV MERCVRE DE FRANCE
XXVI, RVE DE CONDÉ, XXVI

—

MCMIV

à Madame Willy, un
poète qui n'a pas été um
plus primé.
1904.

The year 1905 marked the crest of Willy's extraordinary celebrity. Under his aegis, there appeared a 290-page book called *Willy et Colette,* containing pictures, caricatures, articles, even a bibliography. Colette's portrait was painted by Jacques-Emile Blanche (it now hangs in Barcelona's Museum of Modern Art). Boldini's portrait of Willy was shown in the 1905 Salon. The couple were photographed on horseback in the Bois de Boulogne and *chez eux,* at a joint writing table.

And behind the public image, Colette continued her anonymous chore. "A prison is indeed one of the best workshops. I know what I am talking about: a real prison, the sound of the key turning in the lock, and four cloistered hours before I was free again. 'Show your credentials!' What I had to show were so-many well-filled pages."

🌷 On September 17, 1905, Colette's father, "so young at seventy-six," died
at Châtillon-Coligny. As with Sido, Colette did not write about him for over
a decade. Then, in the short sketches of her childhood in *La maison de
Claudine,* and later in *Sido,* she portrayed him as easily the most gallant and
impetuous lover in her entire male *dramatis personae:* "I never surprised my
parents in a passionate embrace . . . But once, on a summer day, when my
mother was removing the coffee tray from the table, I did see my father bend
his graying head and bearded lips over my mother's hand with a devotion so
ardent and ageless that Sido, speechless and as crimson with confusion as I,
turned away without a word . . . It did me good to behold, and every now
and again to remember afresh, that perfect picture of love: the head of a man
already old, bent in a kiss of complete self-surrender on a graceful, wrinkled
little hand, worn with work."

❧   A characteristic publicity photograph of 1905 shows Colette in a Claudine collar, with Willy's top hat and the living original of Toby-Chien.

1 9 0 6 – 1 0

L'Envers du Music-Hall

Les artistes de café-concert . . . Qu'ils sont
mal connus, et décriés, et peu compris!

How unrecognized, how disparaged, how little-
understood our music-hall artists are!

COLETTE, *La vagabonde*

✤ By early 1906, Colette had made two major moves that were to change her public and private life forever. On February 6 came her professional debut as a mime, playing the role of a faun in a drama called *Le désir, l'amour et la chimère,* by Francis de Croisset and Jean Nouguès. A month earlier, she had left Willy, settling for the first time into an apartment all her own, at 22, rue de Villejust, half a block away from the newly married Paul Valéry, and just around the corner from 2, rue Georges-Ville, the address of a lady in her early forties, "from the highest strata of society," known to her intimate friends as Missy, a lady who was to be Colette's close companion and lover for the next five years and whom a short story called *"Nuit blanche"* tenderly evokes: "Bent over me, your eyes filled with maternal anxiety, you offer me sensual love, seeking in your passionate friend the child you have never had."

❦ Missy—known to readers of *Le pur et l'impur* as La Chevalière—was born Sophie-Mathilde-Adèle de Morny (1863–1944). She was the niece of Napoleon III and the great-granddaughter of the Empress Josephine. After a brief marriage to the Marquis de Belboeuf, she lived alone on rue Georges-Ville, where "dressed in a mechanic's overalls, she turned out bathroom fixtures on a lathe," and where she kept a salon for ladies of the powerful sapphic underground to which French law, or at least the Prefect of the Paris Police, obliged women who preferred men's attire and each other's company to resort. It was here, in an ambience of "fine wines and long cigars," that Colette encountered the "baronesses of the Empire, canonesses, lady cousins of the Tsar, illegitimate daughters of grand-dukes, exquisites of the Parisian bourgeoisie, and also some aged horsewomen of the Austrian aristocracy, hand and eye of steel," who constituted the Tout-Paris of Gomorrah and whom, in *Chéri* and *Ces plaisirs* . . . , she was to portray so vividly.

❦ The ex-Marquise de Belboeuf, as a man. "The lady of the house, in dark masculine dress, belied any idea of gaiety or bravado. Pale, without blemish or blush, pale like certain antique Roman marbles that seem steeped in light, the sound of her voice muffled and sweet, she had all the ease and good manners of a man, the restrained gestures, the virile poise of a man . . . her title and name alike clashing with her stocky masculine physique and her reserved, almost shy manner."

❦ "Mathilde de Morny," says an inscription in Colette's handwriting, "who made herself a pair of mustaches with the help of her chestnut-colored poodle's tail."

❧ It was about this time that Colette was reported to be wearing a bracelet engraved: *"J'appartiens à Missy* . . . I belong to Missy."

❧ The summer of 1907 found them sharing Missy's villa in the seaside resort of Crotoy, in Picardie, with Willy and his current mistress living next door. Later summers were spent in Brittany, near Saint-Malo, where Missy bought another house. A journalist named Maurice Martin Du Gard has recalled a visit: "I had come without warning, but I had a letter of introduction to the ex-marquise, with whom Colette was then living. As I pushed open the gate, I noticed a man coming down the drive toward me, a middle-aged gentleman with pince-nez, short gray hair, a paunch, and wearing white trousers and a black alpaca jacket. I handed him my letter of introduction, and to my great surprise, he opened and read it. This gentleman, it turned out, was the marquise."

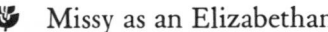 Missy as an Elizabethan

❧ Colette *en travesti*

🌢 Missy and Colette keeping in condition.

"The seduction emanating from a person of uncertain or dissimulated sex is powerful . . . Anxious and veiled, never exposed to the light of day, the androgynous creature wanders, wonders, and implores in a whisper . . . Its half equal, man, is soon frightened and flees. There remains its other half equal, a woman. There especially remains for the androgynous creature the right, even the obligation, never to be happy. . . ."

❧ Natalie Clifford Barney (1876–1972) and Renée Vivien (1877–1909)—posing here in Directoire clothes—were two of the best-known members of Paris–Lesbos at the turn of the century. Both were writers: Barney a tart aphorist and autobiographer, as well as the addressee of Remy de Gourmont's *Lettres à l'Amazone;* and Vivien, whose real name was Pauline Tarn, a poet; and both were beautiful and independently wealthy. But neither, oddly, was French, Barney having been born in the United States and Vivien in England. They were lovers from 1899 to 1905, and at one point they spent a season on the island of Lesbos, hoping to found a colony of homosexual ladies in memory of Sappho. At another, during an estrangement, Natalie persuaded soprano Emma Calvé to sing Gluck's aria for grieving Orpheus, *"J'ai perdu mon Euridyce,"* under Renée's window. Exemplary if exhibitionistic, courageous if flagrant, they were in their way what we now call culture heroes, who defied prevailing sexual conventions by insisting on their right to behave as foolishly as any heterosexual couple in love.

Colette knew them both intimately in these years ("My husband [Willy] kisses your hands," she wrote Natalie, "and myself all the rest"). Her 1928 portrait of Renée is the best we have of this beautiful, lisping, incorrigibly self-dramatizing child, who bought a daily Buddha and kept the windows of her incense-filled apartment nailed against the perfidies of fresh air. She died at thirty-two, romantically, of voluntary fasting and alcohol. More realistic, Natalie lived to a hale, hearty ninety-six, publishing several volumes of memoirs ("Indiscretion is the privilege of tact," she once said) and earning an affectionate epithet from Colette: *"C'est un chic type* . . . She's a fellow with style."

❦ In its issue for November 17, 1906, a Parisian daily printed the following headline:

THE EX-MARQUISE DE BELBOEUF

PLAYS PANTOMIME

At her town house, a rehearsal of *La romanichelle*. The ex-marquise was quoted as saying that she had acted before, in Spain (and in Spanish), and in Tangier, where she danced the fandango. In Paris, she hoped to give pleasure to a few friends by appearing with Madame Colette Willy. She would use the stage name of Yssim (Missy spelled backwards), and would not be paid.

Present at the rehearsal along with Colette was "the author of *Claudine à l'école*," Willy himself. The reporter admired the ex-marquise's mastery of mime, and especially the ease with which she wore her masculine clothes.

❦ Georges Wague, or Waag (1874–1965), a professional mime who began to give Colette lessons early in 1906. In the following year she began to tour with him and his wife, Christine Kerf, in a succession of eight melodramas until, in 1913, she gave up her regular work on the music-hall stage. He nicknamed her *"Quelle heure est-il? . . . What time is it?"* and in the opening paragraph of *La vagabonde* he appears as Brague, gently teasing Colette for her unprofessional compulsion to arrive early for every performance: "You poor boob of an amateur! You always have ants in your pants. If we listened to you, we'd be putting on our make-up at half-past seven." In 1916, Colette used her influence to obtain him a class in mime at the Paris Conservatoire, and they remained friends for her lifetime.

MOULIN ROUGE

? YSSIM **?**

ET

COLETTE WILLY

DANS

RÊVE D'ÉGYPTE

PANTOMIME DE

Mme la Marquise de MORNY

Intercalée dans la

REVUE DU MOULIN

2 ACTES 7 TABLEAUX

10 REPRÉSENTATIONS SEULEMENT

Première Représentation le 3 Janvier 1907

LE BUREAU DE LOCATION EST OUVERT POUR CES REPRÉSENTATIONS

❧ The first performance of *Rêve d'Egypte,* "a pantomime by Madame la Marquise de Morny," took place on the stage of one of Paris's most famous music halls on January 3, 1907, and promptly became known as the "scandal of the Moulin Rouge." It was certainly not unprovoked, and Willy was probably its prime organizer. At the very least, it was disingenuous and exploitive to print the Morny coat of arms above "Yssim's" name in the advertising. The Marquis de Belboeuf himself was in the audience, supported by the membership of the Jockey Club, and when Colette and the ex-marquise offered the spectacle of a prolonged, passionate kiss, the house began to clamor. Worse, as the curtain came down, Willy led the applause, in an ambiguous gesture of gallantry or rank cynicism. There were boos, a near riot, and the next day, at the order of the Prefect of Police, the play's title was changed from *Rêve d'Egypte* to *Songe d'Orient* and "Yssim" was replaced by Georges Wague. Even so, the show closed on January 5.

From Châtillon-Coligny, Sido admonished Willy: "It's frightful. Haven't you the authority to forbid your wife's going on the stage?" Willy lost his prestigious position as music critic for the *Echo de Paris,* and Colette, in an interview in *Le Petit Parisien,* hid what must have been her chagrin under a bold show of indignation: "I'm a little dismayed at the cowardice of these gallant gentlemen who didn't hesitate at violence . . . I might have had a bench in my face. It will be their fault if I have to leave the country to earn my living."

❧ Wague and Colette in two scenes from *La chair,* a "maddening mime-drama" which opened November 2, 1907, and ran, in Paris and the provinces, for over 300 performances, until 1911. A program digested the story as follows: "In a smuggler's cabin on the Austro-Hungarian border, the beautiful Yulka [Colette] lives with the fierce smuggler Hokartz [Wague] . . . The latter discovers that Yulka is unfaithful to him with a handsome young officer [usually played by Wague's wife, Christine Kerf]. In a burst of jealousy, Hokartz tries to stab Yulka, but instead his dagger tears her dress, and Hokartz, overwhelmed by her beauty, kills himself."

Half a century later, the film actor Michel Simon was asked what theatrical performance had been the most memorable of his life and he answered without hesitation: "It was in Geneva when I was a young man. I had attended a play which my fellow Swiss liked so little that during the show they kept up a running exchange of jokes and orange peels from one balcony to another. Then suddenly there was a great silence. To what was the city of Calvin rendering such explicit homage? On stage, Colette was in the act of baring her breast."

In the signed photograph, Colette's inscription reads: "Dear Maurice, hide discreetly . . . what I am displaying with such generosity." The dedicatee is Maurice Chevalier.

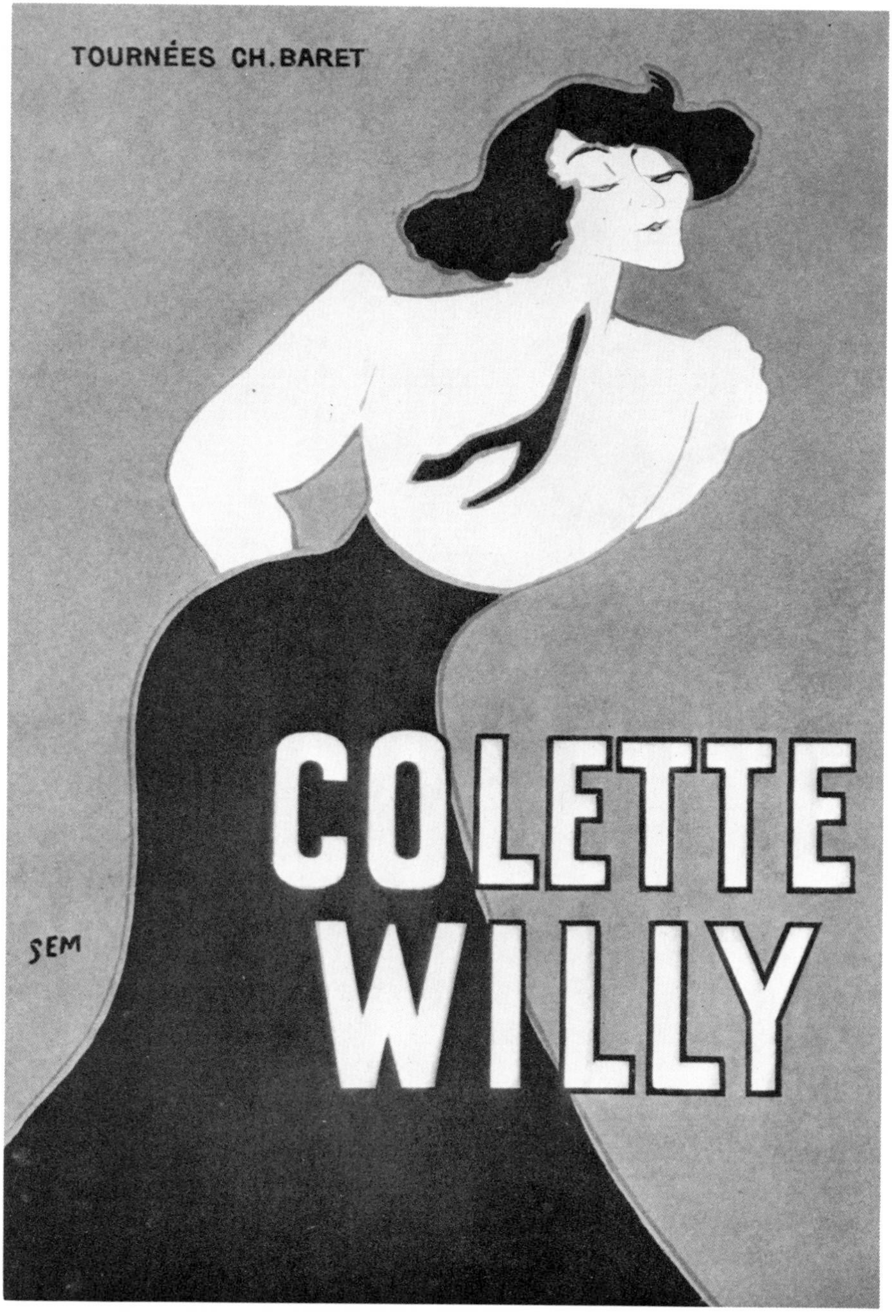
TOURNÉES CH. BARET
COLETTE
WILLY
SEM

By 1909, Colette had appeared not only on the music-hall stage, with Wague's company, but on the legitimate stage as well, first in Willy's adaptation of *Claudine à Paris,* then in a play of her own, *En camarades*. She was now a full-fledged professional, and she had her portrait done by Sem, for reproduction on posters and cards. Acknowledging a copy, Sido somewhat bluntly remarked: "He has caught your posture very well, making your left buttock jut out and your pretty bosom thrust forward."

Holograph copy of the opening paragraph of *Les vrilles de la vigne,* a collection of eighteen short stories, or lyrical sketches, written mostly in dressing rooms and published in 1908. The title piece is an explicitly personal fable about a nightingale which once sang only in the daytime. Then one spring night, while it was sleeping, the tendrils of a neighboring vine slowly wound about its feet, and when it awoke, it was bound fast. It thought it had lost its liberty forever, but finally, with great pain, it wrenched itself free and escaped. All the rest of that spring, and ever after, it swore not to sleep while the vine tendrils were growing. And it was to keep itself awake and alert that it began to sing at night.

❧ Colette examining her poppies in the garden at Mont-Boucons, a small country house in Franche-Comté which Willy gave her in 1902 and then took back after their separation. Under the name of Casamène, a loving portrait of Mont-Boucons appears in *La retraite sentimentale,* a book whose manuscript still reveals Willy's retouching, though it was published in 1907 with only "Colette Willy" on the title page, and a terse notice to the reader: "For reasons which have nothing to do with literature, I have ceased collaborating with Willy. I hope the public which enjoyed our legitimate daughters, the four *Claudines,* will find a little of the same pleasure here."

❧ Colette with Toby-Chien.

On her own now as a writer, Colette made her debut in the smart weekly *La Vie Parisienne* with a new *dialogue de bêtes,* called "Toby-Chien parle," in which her household bulldog and Angora cat gravely discuss their mistress's reaction to the continuing uproar provoked by the Moulin Rouge kiss and the separation from Willy (legalized in February 1907). Colette was thus enabled to offer the reading public her own side of the story. "When I love anything," she tells Toby, "I love it utterly. If you knew how I embellish everything I love, and all the pleasure I get out of loving! If you could understand the wonderful mixture of strength and weakness with which the things I love fill me! It's what I call the caress of happiness."

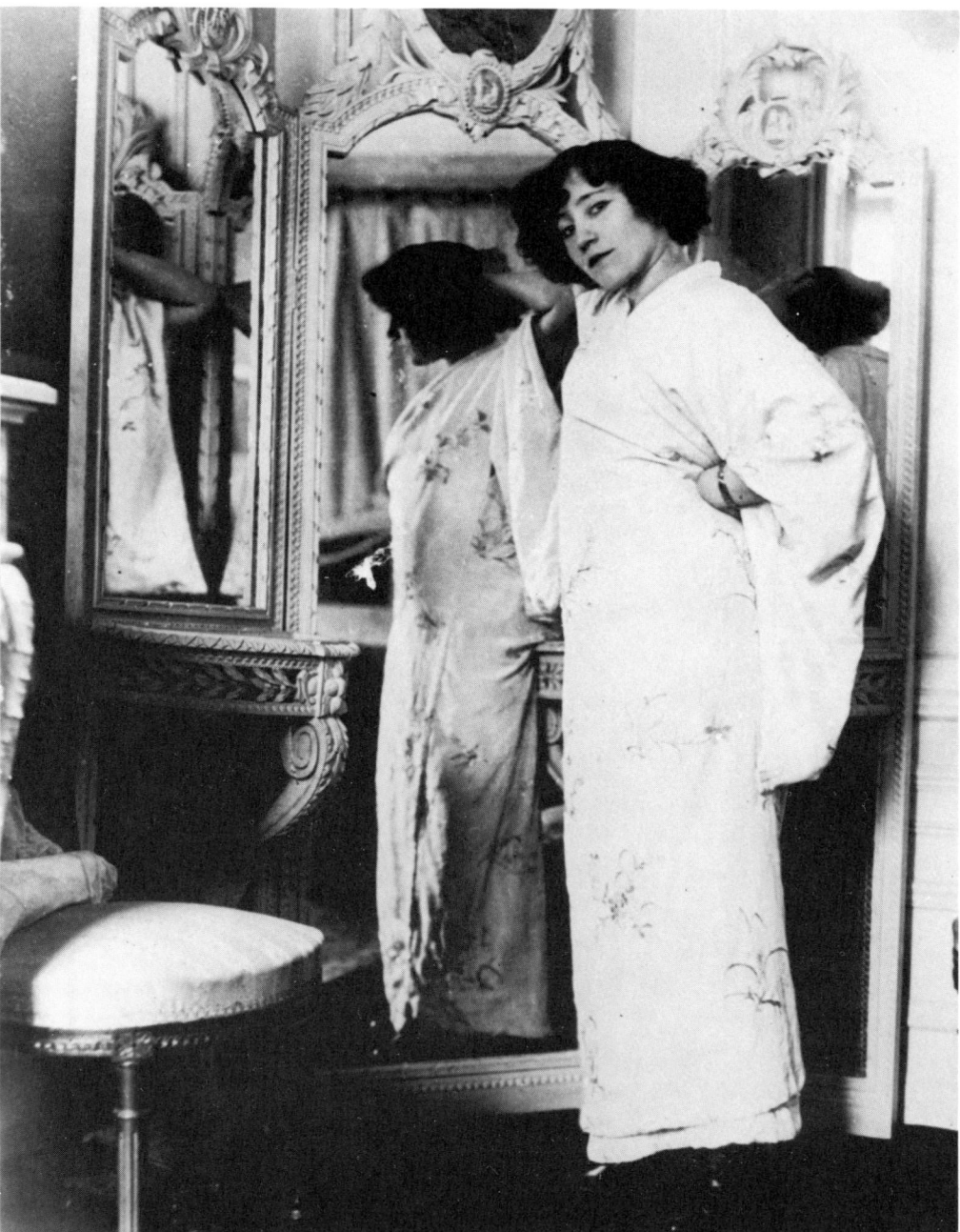

❦ Colette *en miroir.*

Colette continued to appear as frequently in print as on stage. To a new quarterly, *Akadémos,* she contributed notes on butterflies; in *La Vie Parisienne,* she published a tenderly unsinister portrait of her favorite lesbian bar, Palmyre; for her publisher's fall list, she had a novel called *L'ingénue libertine.* At the same time, in Paris, Marseilles, Toulon, she played in *La chair, Claudine à Paris, En camarades.* Then in February 1909 she had bad news. "Without my knowledge, Willy has sold *all* the rights to the *Claudines* for almost nothing, which means that these books, so entirely (morally) mine, are now lost forever. I wrote him, and he replied to my cry of despair with a cold, almost threatening letter."

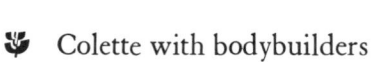 Colette with bodybuilders   Colette in Egyptian costume

🌷 Colette with lion's skin

"Une femme de lettres qui a mal tourné . . . a lady of letters who has gone to the dogs"

❧ Colette in her dressing room. "Involuntarily, I look in the mirror. It is certainly myself I see there, masked in mauve rouge, my eyes ringed with a halo of blue grease paint that is beginning to melt."

❧ Colette in *L'oiseau de nuit,* which opened in August 1911 in Paris. Colette was also responsible for the title

❧ With Georges Wague and Christine Kerf, mugging after a performance of *L'oiseau de nuit*

La Culture Physique

8e Année ❖ N° 165

15 NOVEMBRE 1911

Revue Bimensuelle illustrée
d'Éducation et de Sports
18bis, Rue d'Hauteville, Paris Xe
TÉLÉPHONE 230-45

Le N° 50 Cent.

== Organe de l'Énergie francaise ==

COLETTE
VILLY
fervente adepte de la
CULTURE PHYSIQUE

Photo Reutlinger

🌸 In the title role of *Claudine à Paris*

🌸 Cover girl in November 1911. "Colette Willy, fervent fan of physical culture"

🌷 Colette miming the title role of *La chatte amoureuse,* part of a review called *Ça grise,* at the Ba-Ta-Clan Theater, in April 1912. "I imitate a jealous cat . . . and each time I leave the stage, panting on two heavy paws, with my wool-padded tail dangling from my woman's behind, there, on my dressing-room landing, I meet the concierge's cat, a real Little Cat, who is expressly waiting for me, thin, striped, dressed in velvet. He looks at me for a moment; inclines his cat's face, devilish and charming as a tiger lily; and though he is careful not to laugh, I know he is mocking me."

🌷 Colette, as seen by actor-playwright Sacha Guitry. "The first impression she makes is unfavorable. But soon one feels the charm of her sad, beautiful eyes, and one is amazed to find, when she stops being merely hectic, that there is so much melancholy, so much intelligence, so little naïveté in her."

Samedi 21 Mai 1910 48e année, No 21

LA VIE PARISIENNE
MARCELIN
1863

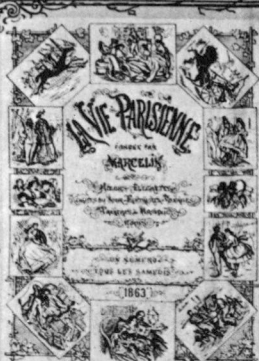

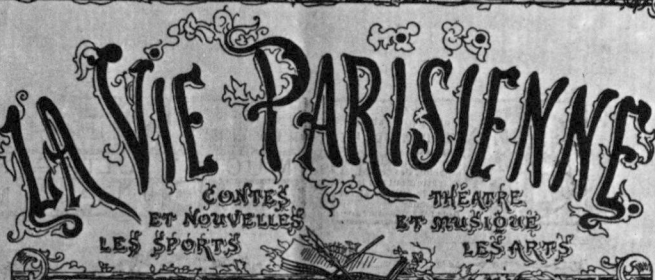

LA VIE PARISIENNE

CONTES ET NOUVELLES — THÉATRE ET MUSIQUE
LES SPORTS — LES ARTS

PARIS ET DÉPARTEMENTS
Un an, 30 francs. Six mois, 16 francs. Trois mois, 8 fr. 50
ÉTRANGER (Union postale)
Un an, 36 francs. Six mois, 19 francs. Trois mois, 10 francs
LES ABONNEMENTS PARTENT DU 1er DE CHAQUE MOIS

PRIX DU NUMÉRO : FRANCE 60 cent. ; ÉTRANGER 75 cent.
RÉDACTION, ADMINISTRATION, PUBLICITÉ
20, boulevard des Capucines. Tél. : 148-59

DANS CE NUMERO COMMENCE :

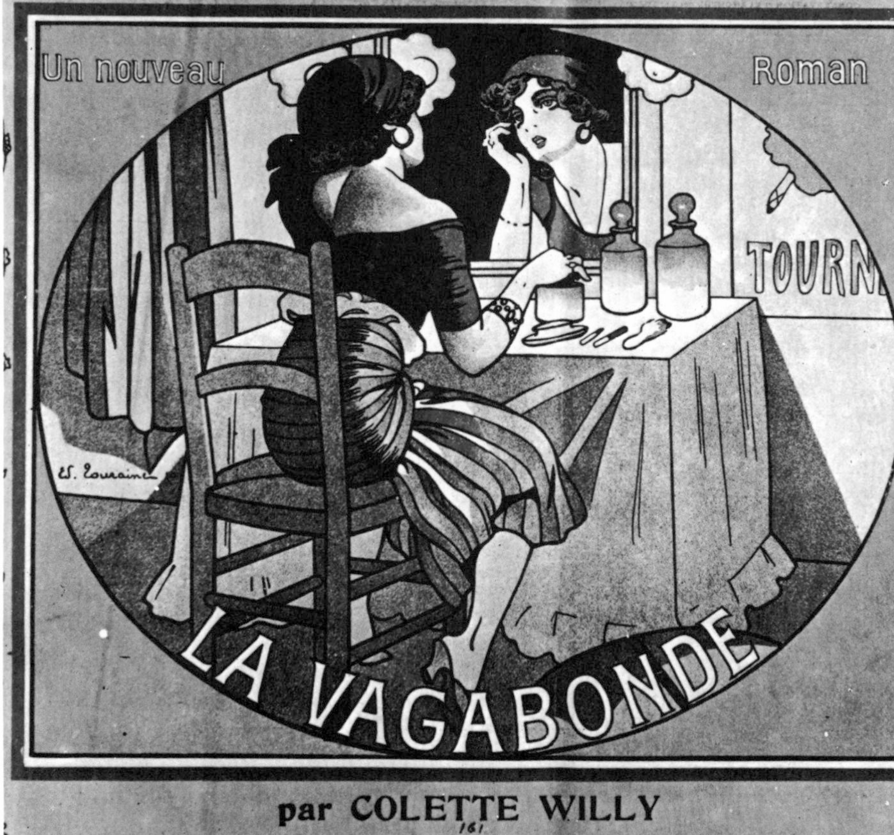
Un nouveau
Roman
TOURN
LA VAGABONDE

par COLETTE WILLY

Cover of the May 21, 1910, issue of *La Vie Parisienne,* in which serialization of *La vagabonde* began. The longest of Colette's novels, it was also the first to be written entirely on her own. Renée, a divorced lady of letters, dances to earn her living. A wealthy young Prince Charming appears and offers to take her away from it all. Renée is tempted, but in the end opts for her freedom. The book is transparently autobiographical, yet there is none of that "facile effusion and poetic swooning" which Gide scorned "in most women writers." Colette's most intimate lyricism is under strict control, and "her own severity very happily disarms the critic . . ." Willy had been a bad husband, but a good writing master, and no matter how much Colette's apprenticeship had cost in chagrin, it now began to pay off in artistic self-knowing and creative finesse. There is not a loose line in *La vagabonde:* its text could be shaken out over the floor and not a word would escape.

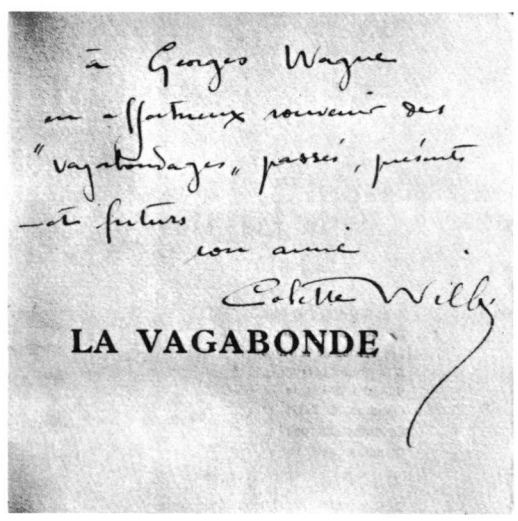

LA VAGABONDE

🌸 The book itself appeared in the late autumn of 1910 (though the copyright page said 1911), and one of the first copies was inscribed to Georges Wague: "In affectionate remembrance of *'vagabondages,'* past, present, and future."

Like so many other books published about this time (*Death in Venice, A Portrait of the Artist as a Young Man, Swann's Way, Sons and Lovers, The Notebooks of Malte Laurids Brigge*), *La vagabonde* has a writer as its central character, and a part of its subject matter is the nature of the literary vocation: "To write is to sit and stare, hypnotized, at the reflection of the window in the silver inkstand, to feel the divine fever mounting to one's cheeks and forehead while the hand that writes grows blissfully numb upon the paper. It also means idle hours curled up in the hollow of the divan, and then an orgy of inspiration, from which one emerges stupefied and aching all over, but already recompensed, and laden with treasures that one unloads slowly onto the virgin page in the little round pool of light under the lamp."

❦ Guillaume Apollinaire (1880–1918), poet, friend of painters, and inventor of the word *"surréaliste,"* shared with Colette a peculiar honor. In December 1910, both *La vagabonde* and Apollinaire's short-story collection called *L'hérésiarque et cie* were candidates for the Prix Goncourt. On the first round, each received three votes, but the prize went to someone named Louis Pergaud. "To have had the chance to honor Apollinaire or Colette, and to have let it get away!" (André Billy, in 1956).

🌸 Colette in 1910.

She was still close to Missy. Another frequent companion (and the model for the unsuccessful lover in *La vagabonde*) was Auguste Hériot, heir to the Louvre department-store fortune; and there was also a young lady named Lily de Rême. "These two amorous children are odd by the very fact that they love me. I feed them, tuck them into bed, and take maternal pride in their appetites and good complexions."

But an era in Colette's life was closing. Soon a new métier, new landscapes, new friends, and, above all, a new hero would be entering her world. She was thirty-eight, and acclaim for *La vagabonde* had attracted the attention of *Le Matin,* the leading morning paper in Paris. For the literary page called "Contes des mille et un matins" she was engaged to write semi-monthly stories, but since to most of *Le Matin*'s readers her name was still anathema, her work was to be published under a pseudonym. The first piece, about backstage music-hall life, appeared December 2, signed with a mask. But curiosity as to the author, and admiration for his prose, ran so high that on January 27 the mask was used for the last time, accompanied by a pert avowal, *"C'est moi, Colette Willy."*

1910 – 25

La Fleur de l'Âge

Sois heureuse. C'est une façon d'être sage.

Be happy. It's one way of being wise.

COLETTE, in a letter to Musidora

Henry Bertrand Léon Robert, Baron de Jouvenel des Ursins (1876–1935), traced an illustrious lineage back to the fourteenth-century magistrate of Troyes, Juvénel des Ursins, and to the Orsini family of Rome. He was "handsome, envied, intelligent" (Colette), as well as gallant and seductive, with a gift for both the written and the spoken word. When he met Colette, he was thirty-six, editor-in-chief of *Le Matin,* father of two sons, Bertrand and Renaud, and no longer married. Their initial encounters doubtless took place in the editorial offices of *Le Matin* on the boulevard Poissonnière. Then at Easter 1911, according to one memorialist, they were guests at the same house party in Compiègne. Colette had come with Auguste Hériot. Henry—or Sidi, as he was known to intimate friends—had for two years been attached to the hostess, Madame de Comminges ("La Panthère"), the mother of his

younger son. Ten days later, Colette and Henry returned to Paris together, and
by the beginning of May, Colette was writing to Wague from Missy's house
in Brittany: "What an arrival! It's hard—it's arrangeable but it's hard!" What
was hard was the sudden presence in her life of Sidi. Missy had been able to
contain Hériot and Lily de Rême. But Henry de Jouvenel was a serious threat.

🌺 Castel-Novel, the Jouvenel family seat in Corrèze. "Roses and nightingales
are flourishing, even the strawberries are beginning to ripen. And what roses!
The house, the walls, the gardens are all covered . . . I have never seen so
many, nor such varieties. It's a horticultural explosion of roses. The more one
cuts, the more they bloom."

❧   Missy. If at any point in Colette's life her personal history resembled the sort of melodrama she mimed on stage, it was in July 1911; a letter of the 31st to Léon Hamel recapitulates the intricate plot with nimbleness, panache, and winning self-awareness:

> You know that Jouvenel dropped in, declaring that he could not and would not live any longer without me, but do you know that, upon returning to Paris, he declared to La Panthère that he loved another woman? Whereupon she declared that she would kill that woman, no matter who it might be. Alarmed, J. warned me of this threat, to which I replied: "I'll go to see her."
>
> And I go, and I tell La Panthère, "I'm the woman," whereupon she melts and implores. A passing weakness, for two days later she announces to J. that she intends to knife me. Realarmed, J. accompanies me to Rozven, where we find Missy, glacial and disgusted, having just heard from La Panthère.
>
> Meanwhile, Jouvenel is having his house fitted up for me. He is without a fortune, but he has *Le Matin* (forty thousand or so francs), and since I earn a good living, we will manage. Need I tell you again that I love this man, who is tender, jealous, unsociable, and incurably honest? Missy is still glacial and disgusted, and no matter what I do, I can't get a sensible word out of her.

Eclipsed by Sidi, Missy receded into the background of Colette's life, though they remained friends. She died in June 1944, a few weeks before the Liberation of Paris, after an attempt at suicide. Her fortune was gone, she had begun to lose her memory, and it was only thanks to Sacha Guitry that she had enough to eat. "*Sa fin de vie,*" wrote Colette, "*n'a rien de gai* . . . The end of her life had nothing gay about it."

❧   As reporters for *Le Matin*, Colette and Henry de Jouvenel were aboard
the dirigible *Clément-Bayard* when it made a trial ascent in June 1912. In
September, they ventured up in a balloon. It was a novel experience, of
course, but in retrospect Colette always preferred the earth to the air. "From
my first flight, I found it boring up there. Either one is terrestrial or one
isn't." Coming back down, she gratefully noted an invisible point at which
the odors of the earth are perceptible again, along with bird cries, church
bells, and human voices.

   As she had written novels under the aegis of Willy, so Colette now began
a new career in personal journalism under the editorship of Henry de
Jouvenel. And for the rest of her long life as a professional writer, she was to
excel at this particular form—a chronicle of some two or three thousand
words in which a character called Colette records her impressions of a myriad
of subjects: murderers on trial, visits of crowned heads, a school for blind
children, the maiden voyage of the *Normandie,* politicians, painters, sports
events, holidays, birds, beasts, and flowers, every aspect of *la mode*, and the
food, weather, and landscapes of France in all seasons. Half of her *Oeuvres
complètes* is made up of those fresh, intimate, precisely observed *chroniques,*
and it was in acknowledgment of their importance in her lifework that the
critic Jean Paulhan once described her as "our best journalist, who somehow
strayed into the novel."

❧ Sido did not approve of her daughter's new métier. "You're going to write an article every eight days for *Le Matin*? But that's too much. I deplore it. Journalism is the death of a novelist." She felt something analogous about Colette's relationship to Henry de Jouvenel. When he invited her to visit Colette and himself in their new ménage in the rue Cortambert, she declined, explaining that her pink cactus, which flowered every four years, was about to blossom and that at her age . . . To Colette she was less elusive:

"I preferred, yes, really, I preferred the other one."

"But, Mother! Willy was an imbecile!"

"Yes, yes . . . But you wrote beautiful things with the imbecile . . . With this one, you'll spend your time bringing him all your most precious gifts . . . But, fortunately, you are not in too much danger."

Then, on September 25, 1912, aged seventy-six years and eleven months, Sido died in Châtillon-Coligny. "I don't want to attend the burial," Colette wrote. "I'm telling almost no one and I shall not wear any visible mourning . . . But I am tormented by a stupid notion: that I shall not be able to write to her any more . . ." With the exception of a few postcards, all of Colette's letters to Sido were destroyed by her brother Achille's wife, that same year.

Samedi 15 Mars 1913

51ᵉ Année, Nᵒ 11

LA VIE PARISIENNE

CONTES
ET NOUVELLES
LES SPORTS

THÉATRE
ET MUSIQUE
LES ARTS

PARIS ET DEPARTEMENTS

ÉTRANGER

RÉDACTION, ADMINISTRATION, PUBLICITÉ
29, rue Tronchet (8ᵉ) : Tél. 148-59

Dans ce numéro commence

L'ENTRAVE

PAR

COLETTE WILLY

❦ By December, another novel was under way, a sequel to *La vagabonde*. At first it was called *Le raisin volé,* but when it began to appear in *La Vie Parisienne,* it was titled *L'entrave.* The heroine-narrator is still Renée, the hero is modeled on Henry—or at least on Colette's feelings for him—and the theme is bondage. Renée can no longer choose to be an unattached drifter. She is in love, and love entangles, binds, shackles. "It seems, as I watch him fling himself at life, that he has taken my place, that he is now the eager vagabond, and I have become his watcher, anchored at his side forever."

The "shackle" became legal in December 1912. Less than three months after Sido's death, Colette found herself pregnant, and at 4:30 p.m. on December 19, in the town hall of the 16th arrondissement of Paris, she became the Baronne de Jouvenel des Ursins. "It's fantastic but obligatory: you have to declare your age!" Colette was to be forty the following month.

❧ On July 3, 1913, at 57, rue Cortambert, and after an exhausting thirty hours of labor, Colette gave birth to a second Colette: "a new person who had entered the house without coming in from the outside." Serialization of *L'entrave* was interrupted, then resumed in October. But Colette was never satisfied with the ending, which she thought cramped and skimpy. She also felt uncertain about, not her daughter, whom she adored, but her own motherhood. "Whenever Sido found me doing needlework as a child, she would shake her head. 'Whatever you do, you'll never look like anything but a boy who's sewing.' And if she could see me now, she'd say, 'You'll never be anything but a writer who has made a child.' She, canny Sido, would not have been unaware of the accidental nature of my maternity."

❧ Colette de Jouvenel II, at ten months.
No one in Colette's circle seems to have escaped a pet name. As her mother was Sido, her father the Captain, her brothers the Savages, her husbands Willy and Sidi; as she herself was Minet-Chéri as a child; so now her daughter became known, not only to family members, but to thousands of her mother's readers, as Bel-Gazou . . . Beautiful Gazelle.

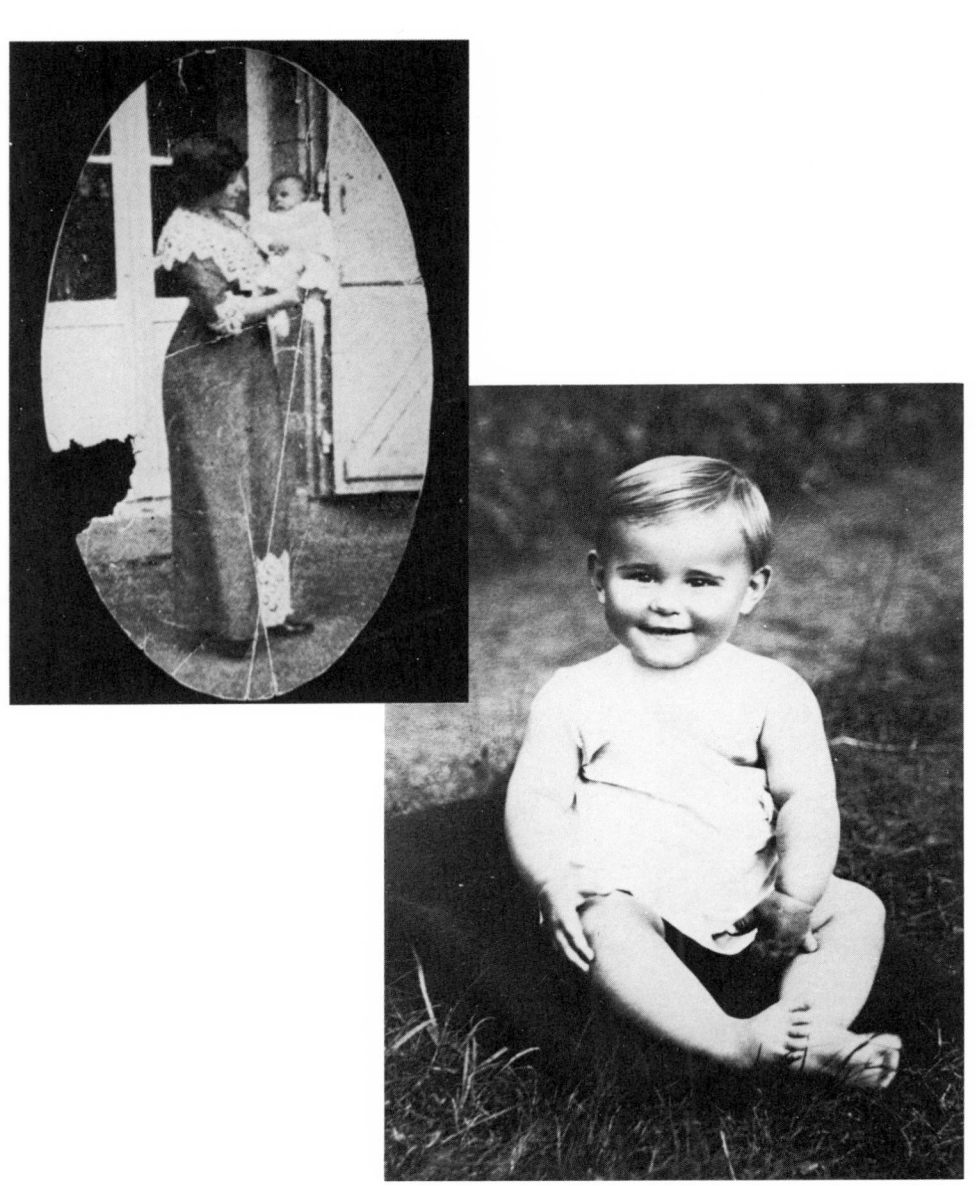

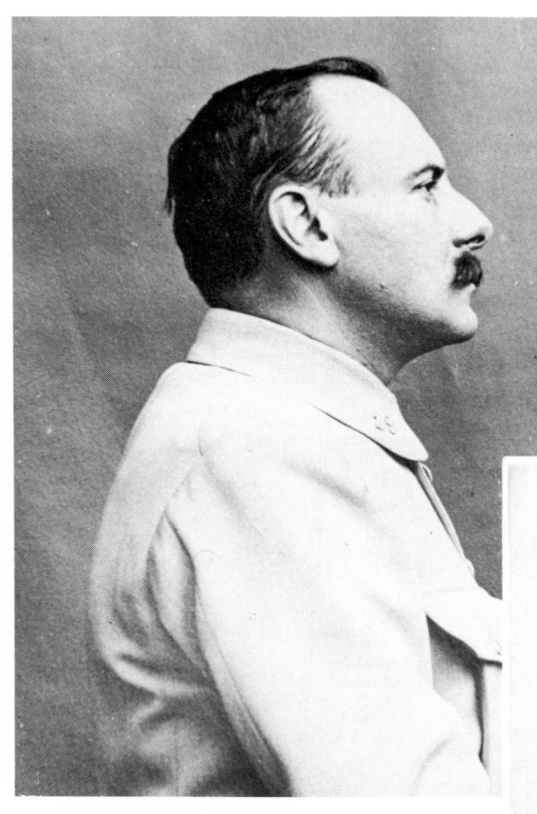

L'Éclair

Journal de Paris, Quotidien.
Politique & Littéraire

ADMINISTRATION

10, RUE DU FAUBOURG-MONTMARTRE, 10

TÉLÉPH. { ADMON : GUTENBERG 02-14
RÉDACON : » 02-25

Mardi, 2 avril

Mon amour, tu ne
reçois pas non plus mes lettres.
Nous sommes de pauvres animaux.
J'ai ton mot de Samedi,
j'en suis bien contente. J'ai
encore eu mille enfants
hier, enfin une trentaine.
Mon amour, on nous a
encore réveillés cette nuit
un abondant tir de barrage,
de 2 h ½ à 4 heures. C'est

❦ Henry de Jouvenel in uniform.

When war broke out in August 1914, Henry promptly enlisted as a sergeant, and Colette served as a night nurse in a Paris military hospital. In December, she contrived to smuggle herself through the lines to join Henry at Verdun, spending New Year's Day in the Argonne and describing her adventures for what had now become a weekly "Journal de Colette" in *Le Matin*. Henry remained in uniform throughout the war, though he was on leave to serve on a diplomatic mission in Italy in 1917. In 1918, promoted to lieutenant, he was cited for "courage, devotion, and remarkable sangfroid under fire."

❦ Part of a letter from Colette to Henry, dated Tuesday, April 2 (1915). "My love . . . we were awakened again last night by bombardment from two-thirty to four. Two shells hit near *Le Matin*'s offices."

In spite of the nightly danger from the zeppelin raids, these were what Colette called *"les beaux jours du phalanstère* . . . the great days of the phalanstery." Bel-Gazou was safely tucked away in Corrèze with an English nanny, and three close friends—Marguerite Moreno, the actress Musidora, and the journalist Annie de Pène—were sharing Colette's chalet-like house in the rue Cortambert. "Musidora did the shopping and cooking . . . I swept and washed. What a squad of women! And the most beautiful peaches in Paris cost five sous."

✤ Colette in Venice, July 1915, with a friend, M. Conneau de Beaumont. Italy entered the war in 1915, and Colette was sent to Venice and Rome as a special reporter. Characteristically, she noticed the number of pregnant women; in France they were scarce, since most of the potential fathers had been mobilized for a year. "And the men here," she added. "Handsome men, and handsome *young* men, not one of whom, moreover, is unaware of his virtues."

❦ Colette and Henry in Rome, winter–spring 1917.
While Henry attended diplomatic conferences and visited the Italian front, Colette put together a selection of her wartime reportages, called *Les heures longues*. Since *L'entrave,* three other collections of short pieces had appeared in book form: stories of backstage life, in *L'envers du music-hall;* portraits of cats and dogs, in *Prrou, Poucette et quelques autres;* and intimate glimpses of a whole gamut of animals—hoot owls, butterflies, fish, snakes, leopards, panthers—in *La paix chez les bêtes,* which no less an admirer than Rilke called "a delicious book!"

❧ Colette with Bâ-Tou, her twenty-month-old wildcat from Chad. Colette was never without a pet of some sort—as a very old lady, she spoke of the fire in her grate as a "living beast"—and over the years she had many dogs and cats, as well as a Brazilian squirrel, a swallow, a pair of garden snakes, and Bâ-Tou. "Whenever I come into a room where you are alone with an animal," Henry once said, "I have the sense of being indiscreet." Perhaps it was Colette's relation with Bâ-Tou which prompted this remark. It was a brief but tender intimacy. Bâ-Tou would purr and play like any domestic cat, and loved to have her tummy scratched. But then one day Colette found her dreamily licking the neck of the household puppy, and Bâ-Tou, "innocent of everything except being a wildcat," spent the rest of her days in a Rome zoo. "The Eden permitted us is not a Noah's Ark."

🌿 Colette, Bel-Gazou, and Henry at Castel-Novel, September 1917.
In July 1917, Henry was appointed to a government post, but by September
a ministerial crisis had freed him, and before rejoining his military unit, he
spent a few days with his family in Corrèze. Meantime, Colette had survived
a crisis of her own: on her way to deliver part of a novel-in-progress, *Mitsou,*
to *La Vie Parisienne,* she lost her only copy of the manuscript on the Métro. "I
am not a crybaby, but that evening Sidi found me in bed, shaking, with a
hot-water bottle at my feet, although it was sixty outside. The next morning I
took myself in hand, and reharnessed myself to the most emetic job I've ever
faced in my life, redoing something already finished."

🌿 Still at Castel-Novel: Colette, Bel-Gazou, and one of the family bulldogs,
perhaps the one called Poucette, "because she is very tiny, tiny but strapping."

❧ Musidora (Jeanne Roques, 1889–1957), whom Colette met in 1912 when they played together at the Ba-Ta-Clan Theater. By 1915, Musidora had established herself as a silent-film star in Italy, and it was through her influence that Colette was engaged to write a scenario for *La vagabonde,* filmed in 1916, and then an original scenario the next year, called *La flamme cachée.* Musidora's career lapsed with the advent of sound, but she and Colette remained lifelong friends. In June 1941, Colette described a visit from her:

"She is spending only three days in Paris. She must return to her country place tomorrow because . . .

" 'Because I can't leave the house alone and tomorrow is the day my husband comes to town to see his mistress.' "

❧ Colette, on January 26, 1919, goggled and gloved for the first civil airplane flight since the Armistice.

In June, Colette began to edit as well as contribute to the "Contes des mille et un matins" page; and in December, she took over *Le Matin*'s drama criticism. There were also three more books: *Dans la foule* (1918) assembled sketches of public events; *Mitsou* (1919) evoked a brief romance between a dancer and a young lieutenant on leave (and brought a letter of praise from Proust: "I wept a little this evening as I read Mitsou's last two letters"); and *La chambre éclairée* (1920) gathered stories about Bel-Gazou and the home front during the war.

🌷 The genial manor house of Rozven, overlooking the Brittany coast's Gulf of Saint-Malo, about five kilometers west of the village of Cancale.

Given to Colette by Missy in 1911, it was used for family summer vacations after the war, bringing together Henry and Colette, Bel-Gazou and Miss Draper, her British nurse, Henry's two sons, Bertrand and Renaud, and assorted friends, chiefly those who were also associated with *Le Matin*. The surrounding coast, with its marine life and weather, presently provided the background for Colette's novel *Le blé en herbe*.

🌷 Colette at Rozven. "If you would know her, think of a garden in Brittany, by the sea. It is early morning and she has been awakened by the melancholy two-note whistling of those birds we call *courlis* [curlews]: she has come down, carefully bypassing a stack of sleeping cats, and the bulldog has followed her silently. She sits in delightful loneliness on the damp and salty grass and her hand enjoys the roughness of the herbs. The sound of the waves fills her mind; she looks now at them, now at the flowers, which are moving faintly upward as the weight of the dew dissolves. The earthly paradise is here: it is not lost for her; others merely fail to see it."

❧ Bertrand de Jouvenel, Colette, and Francis Carco, at Rozven.
Born in 1903, Bertrand was Henry's oldest child and, as Colette's "bookish
foster son," an intermittent member of her household from 1919 to 1925. His
portrait appears under his own name in one of Colette's sweetest short stories,
"Le veilleur," and he may have contributed generic traits to the teenaged hero
of *Le blé en herbe.* Colette has described him, about this time, as "an imitation Musset, with a crazy mop of blond, unwashed hair, wild-eyed,
charming, irresponsible, and affected."

Francis Carco (François Carcopino, 1886–1958) was a Corsican born in
New Caledonia, who established himself in Paris after 1912 with a series of
novels celebrating *la vie de bohème* of Montmartre. Henry de Jouvenel coined
the word *"carcoise"* to identify his world of tender-tough pimps and pros-
titutes, *apaches* and *bals-musettes.* He met Colette about 1918 and they remained friends for life. In his memoirs he describes occasionally escorting
her to the lowly milieus he was an authority on. "The most savory remark I
ever heard in one of those dives was uttered by Colette one night, in a rue de
Lappe *bal-musette* owned by Proust's former valet. After a brutal raid by the
cops, we saw her standing on a table. *'Enfin,'* she cried, *'un peu de rêve . . .*
At last, escape from reality.' "

Renaud de Jouvenel, Bel-Gazou, and her nurse, Miss Draper, at Rozven.

Like his half brother, Renaud (born in 1907) spent his summers at Rozven in the years his father was married to Colette. He, too, appears in her short story *"Le veilleur,"* and was described at thirteen as "sealed off, looking inside . . . a tough little poet who would have died rather than admit he was sad." As Bertrand grew up to become a distinguished economist, Renaud became a poet. He even has a place in American literary annals as the French translator of Randall Jarrell.

Miss Draper was Bel-Gazou's English governess from 1913 to 1921. "How can I ever forget," wrote Colette years later, "that during the length of the war a cantankerous foreigner, hard on herself and everyone else, consented to live in the country, alone with a small child, defending what I possessed, alternately gardener, doctor, and cook, and then refused any wages?"

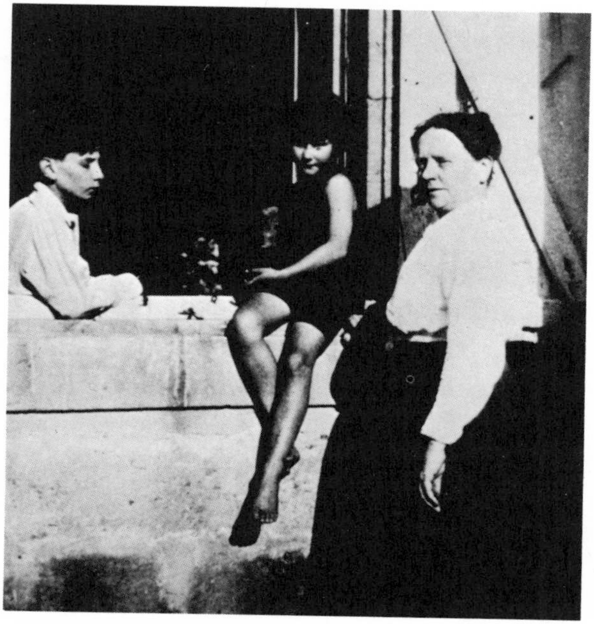

Colette in 1920, the year of *Chéri*.

Chéri began with eight short stories written for *Le Matin* in 1911–12. In the earliest, Chéri was called Clouk. He was young, rich, insecure, and his "name derived from the tiny, though intolerable clicking noise made by one of his blocked nostrils every time he took a breath." But Colette could not attach herself to so "quasi-scrofulous a creation," and in January he became Chéri, "glossy as a six-month-old tomcat . . . with a chest like a breastplate and, oh, those teeth!" It was in this incarnation that he reappeared exactly eight years later, when his story began to run as a weekly serial in *La Vie Parisienne*. The book was published in July, and in December, Colette received a letter from André Gide:

> Madame,
>
> I have devoured *Chéri* in a single gulp. What an admirable subject you have undertaken, and with such intelligence, such mastery, such understanding of the least avowed secrets of the flesh! From beginning to end, not a weakness, not a redundance, not a commonplace . . . But what I love best in your book is its leanness, its clean divestment, its nudity.

Suzanne Derval, whom Colette knew in her music-hall years and whom she herself identified as the model for Léa. As for Chéri: "I could not say that he resembled anyone in particular. But I would be lying if I said that he resembled no one."

Colette *chez elle,* 69, boulevard Suchet.
While the war was still in progress, and her family dispersed, Colette had moved from the chalet in Passy to a private house in Auteuil, adjoining the Bois de Boulogne. Here, as Madame de Jouvenel, she entertained the leading statesmen of the day, and here, as Colette, she finished *Chéri* and continued her multiple activities on *Le Matin*. In September 1920, she was named Chevalier de la Légion d'Honneur, a rare distinction for a woman at this time, and described some of the rewards in a letter to Francis Carco: "Sapène [director of *Le Matin*] gave me a dinner, Sarah Bernhardt sent me a telegram, and Sidi and the three offspring organized a parade at Castel-Novel, requisitioning all the armor and ghosts in the house . . . the children even tied my writing materials in red ribbon."

❧ Novelist Germaine Beaumont at the time she was Colette's secretary at *Le Matin*.

One of Colette's dearest friends, Annie de Pène, had been a victim, in 1918, of the influenza epidemic which assailed Western Europe, and her orphaned daughter, Germaine Beaumont, became the first of a number of fledgling writers—Hélène Picard, Claude Chauvière, Renée Hamon, Bel-Gazou herself—whom Colette took under her wing and encouraged.

About the same time, journalist Maurice Martin Du Gard visited Colette's office at *Le Matin*. There was an autographed photograph of D'Annunzio on the wall, and another of Verlaine drinking absinthe. Colette was speaking on the telephone when young Martin Du Gard was shown in. "She noticed me, made me an imperious and severe sign to enter, and with the same bare arm offered me a box of chocolates. 'My pralines—which ought to be good enough for you!' and her fox muzzle burrowed into the mouthpiece again. 'No, no, my dear. I wasn't talking to you. My chocolate pralines aren't for you. You don't deserve them! They're for a young admirer. Yessss . . . of my prose, of course.'

"Hanging up, she sighed, collapsed on her desk, arms crossed, shoulders heavy . . . But a glint of mischief, subtle and cruel, briskly reanimated her eye, and she seized her pocketbook, emptying out pell-mell her powder box, rouge, lipstick, key ring, and finally photographs of Bel-Gazou. 'My daughter! Look at her, my boy! She's the best thing I've ever made!' "

❧ Hélène Picard (1873–1945) was a poet and short-story writer who came to *Le Matin* as another of Colette's protégée-secretaries around 1920. "A life as pure as hers cannot fail to appear mysterious," Colette wrote later. "She lived on three mountaintops: chastity, pride, poverty." She was also prone to violent, high-minded bursts of anger (after which she would say, "Pay no attention, Colette. It's my time of day to frighten children") and to obstinately ingenuous views: "Hélène would become quiet, even inhibited, before a question of homosexual relations. She even refused to admit their existence. Of two women who played man and wife, and whom the rest of us regarded without severity, she exclaimed: 'No, no, it's ugly. Or rather, it's laughable . . .' But when one of us pointed out that the opposite sex neither eschewed nor disdained analogous variants, she softened. 'Oh, it's all right between boys . . .' and refused to explain any further." Increasingly aloof and reclusive as the years passed, she lived in a fourth-floor walk-up decorated entirely in azure blue, including a pair of parakeets, which one of her poems called the "frivolous favorites of somber mariners . . ." Colette worried about her, obtained advances for her from publishers, and always regarded her as a great poet, especially for a 1927 volume called *Pour un mauvais garçon*.

🌿 Henry de Jouvenel.

His brief taste of government service in 1917 prompted Henry to present himself as a senatorial candidate from his native Corrèze in 1921, and in January he was elected. During the campaign, when one of his opponents spread the rumor that he was married to a dancer, his only response was to take Colette electioneering. Again, after the election, when he was invited by Poincaré to dinner at the Elysée Palace, he replied that he would be happy to call on the President of the Republic but that he dined every evening with Madame de Jouvenel. Poincaré hastened to reword his invitation.

❧ Colette at the trial of the murderer Landru, in November 1921.

A small book could be made of Colette's writing as a crime reporter. From 1912, when she attended the trial of a certain "Houssard, accused of having killed, and Madame Guillotin, accused of having loved," through 1939, when she covered the trial of Weidman, the last man to be publicly guillotined in France (and immortalized in the opening sentence of Genet's *Notre-Dame-des-Fleurs*), she brought to courtrooms the same unsentimental yet empathic watchfulness which she brought to plants, animals, weather, lovers, and her own psyche. Studying Landru, who had murdered a succession of wives, she fixed on his eyes: "I look in vain for human cruelty in these eyes, because they are not human. They are bird's eyes . . . and when Landru half lowers his lids, his look takes on the languor, the unfathomable disdain of caged wild birds . . . I look further for evidence of the monster but I don't find it. If this face is frightening, it is because it has that air of perfectly imitating human beings which one finds in the immobile mannequins of clothing-store windows."

❧ Colette with her *brabançonne* bitch Pati, who appears in *La maison de Claudine* and *Le fanal bleu,* and as one of the principal characters of *Bella-vista,* a sort of murder mystery in which Pati detects the villain's identity before anyone else. "She was called Pati when it was necessary for us both to be on our best behavior. When it was time for her walk, she was Pati-Pati-Pati, or as many more Patis as one had breath to add. Thus we had adapted her name to all the essential circumstances of our life."

❧ Colette in the garden of her Auteuil house, 1922.

For two years Colette had been drawing upon her Saint-Sauveur childhood for her weekly stories in *Le Matin,* and now, a decade after Sido's death, she gathered thirty of them into a book, *La maison de Claudine.* In a sense, everything Colette wrote was autobiographical, but this is the first time she approached her parents and their children directly, using their own names. It is also one of Colette's most beautiful books, and therefore a twofold pity that she consented to her publisher's using the old brand name of Claudine in the title. The book should have been called *La maison de Sido,* or even better, as it has come to be known in its English translation, *My Mother's House.*

❧ Léopold Marchand (1888–1952) was a playwright who collaborated with Colette on stage adaptations of *Chéri* and *La vagabonde.* Describing their working methods, Colette once said, "He writes his scenes reverently, in elegant language, and then I rewrite them, substituting the loose, live, racy speech we use in everyday intercourse . . . If *Chéri* owes much to Léopold Marchand, he in turn will only have learned one thing: how to write inelegantly."

❧ Marcel Proust: "When I was a very young girl, he was a very pretty young man. Trust Jacques-Emile Blanche's portrait."

A little over a year before his death, Proust sent a copy of *Du côté de Guermantes II,* including the beginning of *Sodom et Gomorrhe,* inscribed to "Madame la Baronne de Jouvenel," and Colette acknowledged it with an important avowal of his influence on her own work: *"No one in the world* has written such pages on inversion, but no one! Years ago I wanted to write a study of sexual inversion myself, and it was the substance of your pages that I wanted to express. But my laziness or incapacity failed to get it down."

❧ Georges Simenon began submitting stories to *Le Matin* in the early twenties. "Then one day I was told, 'Madame Colette would like to see you,' and suddenly there she was, marvelous to behold. 'I've read your last story,' she said, 'but it isn't right. It's almost right. It almost works. But not quite. You are too literary. You must not be literary. Suppress all the literature and it will work . . .' That was the most useful advice I've ever had in my life, and I owe a grateful candle to Colette for having given it to me."

🌸 Colette at Rozven, with Francis Carco's wife Germaine, the summer she began *Le blé en herbe*.

Like *Chéri, Le blé en herbe* began as a 2,500-word short story about teenaged Phil and Vinca and a summer spent with their parents on the Brittany coast. Successive chapters appeared from week to week until, by the fifteenth, it was clear that Colette was retelling the story of Daphnis and Chloë and that, as in the Longus original, sexual love would have its way. Indignant readers of *Le Matin* objected and serialization was abruptly suspended. But Colette's professionalism was undaunted and in a single long chapter she brought the story to rest. "Not without torment, however. The last page, those twenty lines, cost me an entire day . . . It's the proportions that give me the greatest trouble. And I have such a horror of grandiloquent finales!"

The book was published in July 1923, and it may have been then that Henry de Jouvenel asked, as Colette's husband as well as senator from Corrèze: "But can't you ever write a book that isn't about love or adultery or rupture or half-incestuous goings-on? Aren't there other things in life?"

🌸 Holograph page from the ninth chapter (pages 78–79) of *Le blé en herbe*. "Artisans, bureaucrats, that's what we writers are! The joys of creation! Novels dashed off in ecstasy in three weeks! Nonsense! Three thousand pages botched and wasted in order to produce two hundred and fifty polished ones."

Colette's earliest books—apart from those signed by Willy alone—were signed "Colette Willy." Beginning with *L'entrave,* in 1913, they were signed "Colette (Colette Willy)." With *Le blé en herbe,* and henceforth, all her books were signed simply "Colette." "And so, before the law, on the printed page, and among my intimates, I have only one name which is my own."

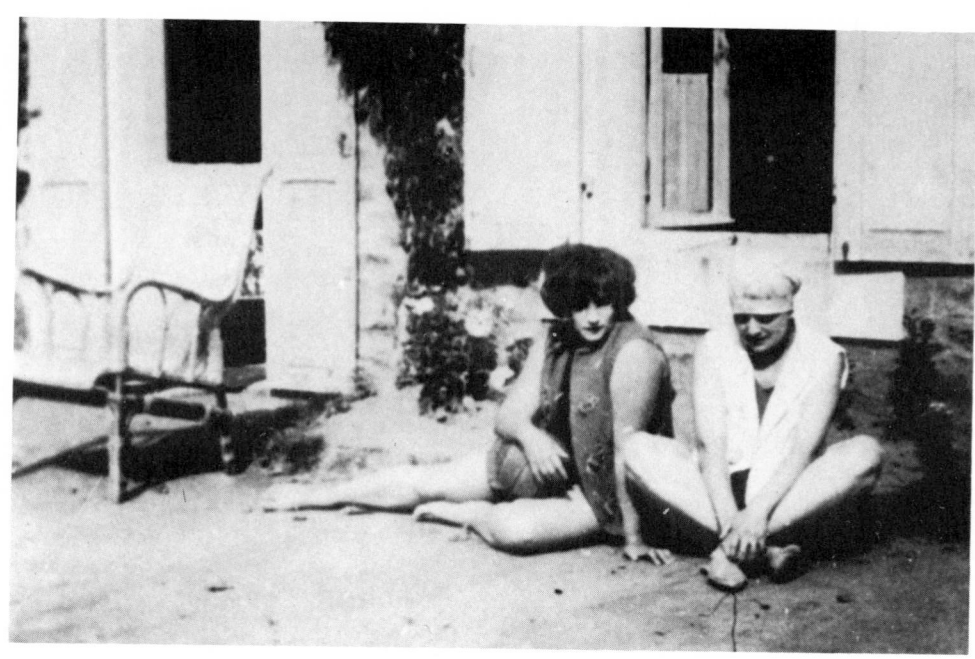

❧ Bel-Gazou with her father, Senator Henry de Jouvenel, in London's Victoria Station.

By the end of 1923, relations between Colette and Henry had hopelessly deteriorated. For one thing, they were two strong, wholly dissimilar personalities ("You cannot imagine what it is like to live with a woman who always has bare feet," Henry used to say, referring to his wife's predilection for sandals). For another, each was dynamically involved in a flourishing career. Over the next decade, Henry was to serve in many diplomatic capacities, as delegate to the Petite Entente, as High Commissioner of Syria, as French ambassador to Rome, as well as publishing books and articles. Colette, in 1923 alone, in addition to her weekly work on *Le Matin,* adapted *La vagabonde* for the stage, appeared with a touring company in *Chéri,* and was in increasing demand as a lecturer. In fact, it was on her return from a lecture tour in December 1923 that she found that Henry "had left without a word." Discreetly handled by Henry's old friend Anatole de Monzie, a divorce was declared final the following year.

❧ Colette on the lecture circuit

❧ Title page for *Aventures quotidiennes*

❧ Advertisement in *La Nouvelle Revue Française* for the "Collection Colette"

"Ah! la, la and again la, la! We are an untold number of women, tormented with anxiety about tomorrow," Colette wrote to Hélène Picard early in 1924, but she knew how to take action against her sea of troubles, and at once. Since Henry de Jouvenel was still affiliated with *Le Matin,* she resigned, and her last column appeared in February. Then, for a magazine called *Demain,* she began in March to write a monthly article on fashion. For the newspaper *Figaro,* she began in April to write a weekly column called "A Woman's Opinion." For one publisher, she put together twenty-two short stories to make a book called *La femme cachée.* For another, she edited a series of books called "Collection Colette." In between, there was a scenario (lost) called *La licorne blanche,* part of an unfinished book for children, stories for the popular weekly *Annales,* further lecturing. When, in October, *Figaro* asked for a biweekly instead of a weekly column, she promptly transferred her services to *Le Quotidien:* "I'm accepting 42,000 francs instead of 60,000, but then there's an extra 2,00 per month for theater reviews during the season." That same month, she collected her twenty-two weekly *Figaro* articles into another book, called *Aventures quotidiennes,* thereby flattering her new employer and putting the discarded one in his place. At this time, she was also trying to begin a new novel, but "it's terrible to think," she wrote Francis Carco, "as I do every time I begin a book, that I no longer have, and never have had, any talent."

COLETTE

Aventures quotidiennes

PARIS
ERNEST FLAMMARION, ÉDITEUR
26, RUE RACINE, 26

COLLECTION COLETTE

Publiée sous la direction de **Colette**

VOLUMES PARUS :

— Il paraît un volume par mois —
Chaque volume sur pur Alfa Outhenin Chalandre.. .. .. **7.50**

FERENCZI et FILS, ÉDITEURS, 9, rue Antoine-Chantin, PARIS

On January 28, 1924, Colette was fifty-one, and she celebrated by spending three weeks with her foster son Bertrand at the Swiss winter resort of Gstaad. "I ski, I skate, I toboggan, I'm behaving like a crazy woman!" Or, as she once said in an interview, "I am never completely unhappy, because I ask so little of life . . . You can't imagine how little it takes to satisfy me."

1 9 2 5 – 4 0

Belles Saisons

Où ne s'est-elle pas fourrée, cette grosse abeille?

Where did our great honey bee not forage?

FRANÇOIS MAURIAC, quoted by Colette in *L'étoile vesper*

❧ Maurice Goudeket (1889–1977) now entered Colette's life, to become her lover for ten years, her husband for nineteen more, and her *"meilleur ami"* for all twenty-nine. Born in Paris, Maurice discovered Colette's writing when he was sixteen and told his parents, "Someday I'm going to marry this woman. Only she will know how to understand me." When they finally met, Maurice was thirty-five, Colette fifty-two. It was at a dinner party, and Colette was barely seated when she snatched an apple from a fruit bowl and took a large bite. "I told myself that she was playing her role," Maurice recalled, "and my suspicion grew." The next time they met, it was Easter 1925, and they were with a group of friends at a hotel on the Cap-d'Ail. Someone said, "Oh, Maurice is always calm . . ." at which Colette threw him a rapid glance and added, "Like a covered flame."

L'enfant
et les
Sortilèges

Maurice Ravel
Colette

❧ Written in eight days, Colette's libretto for *L'enfant et les sortilèges* is about a little boy whose teatime tantrum is at first punished and then forgiven by a host of household objects and garden animals: a Wedgwood teapot, a Chinese cup, a book of fairy tales, squirrels, owls, frogs, cats, dragonflies, an aviary. Ravel's music, interrupted by the First World War, took ten years to write, and the première, complete with the teapot dancing ragtime and two cats miaowing a duet, finally took place in March 1925 in Monte Carlo, opening the following February at the Opéra in Paris. "It's playing twice a week before packed but stormy houses," Colette wrote twelve-year-old Bel-Gazou, away at school. "The partisans of old music will not pardon Ravel his instrumental and vocal daring."

❦ Caricature of Colette as Léa.

"In reality," said one critic, the poetess Gérard d'Houville, "she doesn't act her role so much as she lives it, breathes it, fears it, dissimulates it, suffers it." And playwright Henry Bernstein: "Is Colette a great actress? I don't know. I only know that this is a bantering, haunting, disdainful, cruel, subtle and massive, formidable performance." But André Rouveyre was less easily pleased: "Let Madame Colette make no mistake: the spectator comes out of curiosity about her celebrity as a writer." Backstage, where she was interviewed by Albert Flament, she was "the image of a Renoir with delectable arms . . . In her dressing room, among her pots of make-up and grease paint, cigarettes, fake jewels, letters with importunate demands on perfumed stationery—what a splendid 'crudity' Colette is!"

❧ Colette as Léa, in Act I of *Chéri*. The stage adaptation of *Chéri,* done in collaboration with Léopold Marchand, opened in Paris on December 13, 1921. For the one hundredth performance, in February 1922, Colette herself played Léa, and her success prompted her to repeat the role on various occasions over the next four years. In 1924, she even put together a company consisting entirely of writers.

❧ Colette with Marguerite Moreno, who played the part of Chéri's mother, Madame Peloux. Taken in Nice, in 1925, this is the only known photograph of Colette and her great friend together.

❧ Colette at a wine-tasting in the Côte-d'Or village of Nuits-Saint-Georges, 1925.

"I was very well raised," said Colette. "I was not more than three years old when my father gave me a full glass of reddish-brown muscat de Frontignan, sent from his natal South of France." She also acknowledged that "a difficult page, the conclusion of a novel are advantageously served by an exceptionally well-filled glass." For years, she even made her own wine, as well as something she called *vin d'oranges:* "Into four liters of dry, golden Cavalaire wine, I pour one liter of good, honest Armagnac brandy, and my friends promptly cry out. 'What a massacre! Such a sterling brandy sacrificed to an undrinkable ratafia!' While they are still howling, I drown four sliced oranges, a freshly picked lemon, a stick of silvery vanilla, and six hundred grams of sugar cane. All this goes into a potbellied glass jar, corked and sealed, to macerate for fifty days. Then all I have to do is filter and bottle the result. Is it good, you ask? Just come home at the end of a hard, late-winter afternoon lashed with rain and hail. You are shivering. You feel your forehead, you wipe your nose, you look at your tongue, and finally whimper, 'I don't know what's the matter with me . . .' *I* know what's the matter. You need a little glass of *vin d'oranges.*"

In *La fin de Chéri,* the hero, though still young, rich, in good health, handsome, and well married, shoots himself out of a hopeless lassitude and nostalgia for his first great love, now grown into a stout, cheerful old lady. Colette explained in an interview: "When an older woman has a liaison with a very young man, she risks less than he . . . In all his love affairs that follow, he will be marked, he will never be able to forget the memory of his old beloved."

A "hard, bitter, unsmiling book," it was published early in 1926, while Colette was happily but hectically fulfilling a Paris engagement in *Chéri.* Somehow, when she returned the corrected proofs to her publisher, she accidentally omitted thirty-two pages of printed text, and when the initial printing of 35,000 copies appeared, an entire chapter was missing. In subsequent editions the pages were restored, of course, but Colette was gloomy about the accident for some time. "It was not a question of author's vanity," Maurice Goudeket has explained, "because she actually had none. It was her scrupulousness, her exactitude, her taste for a piece of work well made."

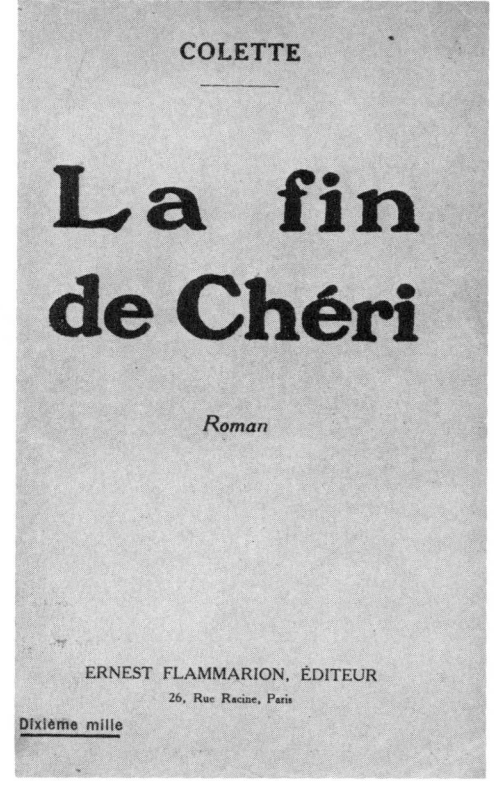

❦ El Hadj Thami Glaoui, the Pasha of Marrakesh, and one of Colette's greatest admirers, was her host when she and Maurice visited Morocco in April 1926. He put one of his palaces at her disposal, and as she wrote to Hélène Picard: "We have been living among colored faïence walls and 'scent gardens,' gardens full of roses, mint, yellow jasmine, daturas, honeysuckle, balm, where the night wind mixes troubling perfumes . . . There is an ancient Arab cemetery nearby where crazily whinnying stallions were pastured this morning, and very close to me, the old russet ramparts are covered with storks."

🌸 Colette, Maurice, and Pati on the terrace of La Treille Muscate in Saint-Tropez, circa 1926.

During the years of her marriage to Henry de Jouvenel, Colette's residential axis had turned on Rozven and the little town house near the Bois de Boulogne. By 1927, in accordance with her new life with Maurice Goudeket, she had replaced both—the Brittany coast with Provence, and the boulevard Suchet in the upper-middle-class 16th arrondissement with the Palais-Royal in the high-bohemian 1st.

In the twenties, Saint-Tropez was not the chic resort it later became, but still a drowsy Mediterranean fishing village with few summer visitors, where one drank white wine in fishermen's quai-side bars and, to Colette's delight, watched "handsome local boys dancing together." Her house, which she called La Treille Muscate (the Muscat Vine), was outside the village, surrounded by a small vineyard and a pine woods, with the Mediterranean just beyond the gate. Here she planted roses and tangerine trees, ate masses of raw garlic ("excellent for the respiratory tracts and against the cold"), and on starry nights slept on the terrace. Here, too, she entertained a small group of mostly painter friends—including Dunoyer de Segonzac, the finest illustrator of her books—wrote and gardened, and generally flourished for thirteen summers. Even after she sold her tiny acreage in 1938, her love affair with the South of France did not lapse, and in the last years of her life she regularly spent the winter in Monte Carlo. "My father," she once observed, "was right to have been born in Toulon."

❧ Colette at her desk in the tunnel-like apartment under the august arcades of the Palais-Royal, where she lived from 1927 to 1930.

"A modest rental, a ceiling I could touch with my hand, and 135 feet of cave-like space . . . I hesitated before such a layout, but nevertheless the day came when I signed a lease and plunged into this tunnel, this sleeve, this drainpipe, this drawer . . . 'Be careful of jumping for joy,' a humorist advised. 'You'll crack your skull.' "

❦ Colette with the cast of *La vagabonde* in the 1927 revival. At left, Léopold Marchand, her co-adapter; and seated, Paul Poiret.

After playing Léa on and off for several years, Colette decided to try the title role of her other play, *La vagabonde,* originally produced in 1923. She invited the illustrious couturier Paul Poiret to play the male lead—hardly an ideal choice, since, however well his name looked on billboards, he could neither look nor act the part. But an otherwise professional cast, including Marguerite Moreno, brought the play to Monte Carlo and Paris early in 1927. Natalie Clifford Barney saw a January performance and described her old friend as a "vagabond indeed, a walking pedestal topped with a tiny triangle of a face, compactly plump, with an octoroon's complexion and the air of an owl in broad light."

❧ Colette with Ninon Gilles and Paul Poiret.

In a letter to Marchand, Colette mentioned her "irritation at having to deal with such an obtuse megalomaniac as Poiret. Moreover, he has no memory, and I have to prompt him *every night.*"

❦ Colette, by Marcel Vertès, one of fifteen lithographs for a limited edition of *La vagabonde* issued in 1927.

"Colette . . . has always given me the impression of a woman who has suffered great wounds in her liaisons . . . She has also impressed me as a highly sensual woman, a bit of a bitch even [*un peu chienne, même*], a woman who wears physical love on her face" (Paul Léautaud).

❧ François Mauriac, who sent Colette a copy of his 1928 biography of Racine inscribed: "To Colette, much closer to this periwigged man than she imagines."

❧ By the late twenties, Colette's reputation was entering a new phase. With the death of Proust, she had come to be regarded as the foremost living stylist in French. Translations of her work into German, English, Spanish, and Italian were beginning to appear. In 1927, there was a sympathetic critical biography by Jean Larnac, and prestigious literary historians, such as René Lalou, now included an evaluation of her work, calling her a "great classic writer." Speaking for the Catholic literary establishment, François Mauriac published an imposing essay on *Chéri* and its sequel, finding them "two admirable books which do not degrade or soil us (*qui ne nous abaissent pas, qui ne nous salissent pas*)," and at a dinner party hosted by Scott Fitzgerald in Baltimore, Thornton Wilder discussed Colette, "saying that there were some of the *Claudine* books that he thought were pretty good" (Edmund Wilson). In March 1926, Colette herself took a significant step. For over a decade, the list of her works opposite the title page of each of her books had sarcastically specified that the *Claudines* had been written *"en 'collaboration' avec M. Willy."* Now she showed an interviewer the original *Claudine* manuscripts and publicly laid claim to their authorship.

La naissance du jour

*"Vous croyez peut-être que
je fais mon portrait ? Patience : c'est
seulement mon modèle. ... mais je « qui est mort ...
... n'est peut-être pas moi... »*

— Marcel Proust

(La naissance du jour)

« *Monsieur,*

« *Vous me demandez de venir passer une*
« *huitaine de jours chez vous, c'est-à-dire au-*
« *près de ma fille que j'adore. Vous qui vivez*
« *auprès d'elle, vous savez combien je la vois*
« *rarement, combien sa présence m'enchante,*
« *et je suis touchée que vous m'invitiez à*
« *venir la voir. Pourtant, je n'accepterai pas*
« *votre aimable invitation, du moins pas*
« *maintenant. Voici pourquoi : mon cactus*
« *rose va probablement fleurir. C'est une*
« *plante très rare, que l'on m'a donnée, et*
« *qui, m'a-t-on dit, ne fleurit sous nos climats*

❧ Corrected proof of first page of *La naissance du jour*.

La naissance du jour is a 40,000-word prose poem to the good life in Provence. It cost Colette desperate hours at her desk: "This is the nth time I have started again on a certain page of my miserable novel [in a letter to fourteen-year-old Bel-Gazou]. I work with ferocious patience, I who am usually so impatient! It's a battle between my two halves. Oh, what a métier writing is! It seems to me that when you've practiced any other craft for over thirty years, you feel a little confidence, a little mastery. With writing, it's the opposite."

Published in March 1928, it is easily Colette's most original novel. The final volume of Proust's *Recherche* had appeared the previous autumn, and its example of meditative narration must have influenced Colette's venturing so relaxed, essay-like a novel, with little or no plot, a self-analyzing narrator called Colette, and the names of actual friends and places woven into the background. She had originally used a quotation from Proust as the book's motto:

Ce "je" qui est moi et qui n'est peut-être pas moi . . . This "I"
which is myself and yet perhaps not myself

But in the proofs she substituted two sentences from page 57 of the book itself:

*Imaginez-vous, à me lire, que je fais mon portrait? Patience:
c'est seulement mon modèle.* . . . Perhaps you imagine I am
drawing my own portrait? Patience: it's only my model.

❧ Colette autographing books. "One always writes for someone. Rarely for several people. Never for everyone."

🌷 Colette with Souci, the last of her bulldogs, who was a household fixture from 1928 until 1939.

"One day Colette said to us: 'I have to go to Saint-Raphaël to buy a refrigerator. I want my butter to be as hard as wood.' That evening she came back, not with a refrigerator, but with a little bulldog bitch. 'She was too sweet,' said Colette. 'I couldn't resist her' " (Segonzac).

🌷 Colette and two of her cats at the time she was writing *La seconde*.

La seconde was published in March 1929. Asked about the book's theme, Colette described it as "austere . . . It's about the solidarity that can exist between two women who are enemies because they love the same man. Imagine the tragic moment when they confront each other . . . If at this moment the man appears, they both want to tell him to get out. He is *de trop,* a stranger, whereas the two women feel a bond."

The book was an immense success, and for Easter, Colette and Maurice went to Spain. In Madrid, they found they had forgotten to make train reservations for Algeciras, so they hired a taxi. When the Baron de Rothschild heard about this, he was shocked. But how much did it cost? he asked. Colette turned to Maurice, who replied: 9,500 pesetas. That's madness, cried the baron, one of the richest men in France. "Why?" Colette exclaimed, "since for once we had the money!"

🌷 Colette in 1929.

Janet Flanner: "She is now a short, hearty-bodied woman with a crop of wood-colored hair, with long, gray, luminous, painted, slanting eyes and a deep alto voice. After years of living in Paris, she still speaks French with a racy Burgundian accent."

Julien Green: "As he arrived, Cocteau showed us a sick bird which he had found in the Champs-Elysées. Colette took it, examined it, and then went out and wrang its neck in the garden."

Pierre Scize: "If we said to her, 'Colette, I am unhappy,' we would hear her voice of a grumbling laborer reply, 'Nobody asked you to be happy. Work. Do you hear me complaining?' "

❦   Radclyffe Hall, author of *The Well of Loneliness,* and her consort, Lady Una Troubridge.

Two of the most controversial books of the twenties were *The Well of Loneliness* and D. H. Lawrence's *Lady Chatterley's Lover.* Colette knew Radclyffe Hall as a member of the group around Natalie Clifford Barney, who had a summer place near Saint-Tropez. "One night there was a new moon over the terrace, and when we became too lyrical, gushing at its thinness and transparency, Colette suddenly brought us back to our senses. 'Come, come now. It looks more like a fingernail clipping.' "

When *Puits de solitude* appeared in France, Colette wrote an acute comment on the earnest self-consciousness of its lesbian heroine. "I feel that if an 'abnormal' person feels abnormal, he is not really so. Wait. I'll put it more clearly: an abnormal man or woman must *never* have the feeling that he or she is abnormal. Just the contrary."

And apropos of "that poor, infantile, excited author of *Lady What's-Her-Name's Lover"*: "It's all so terribly teenaged and sophomoric . . . What a narrow domain obscenity is! One suffocates there at once, and one gets so bored."

However synonymous Colette's name has become with sensuality, there are absolutely no obscene, not even genitally graphic, details in her own work, and the rare occasions of sexual intercourse are purveyed with a gravity and grace that are almost religious.

❦   Claude Chauvière (1895–1939) was another of the young writers who served as Colette's occasional secretary in the twenties. Colette had been her godmother when she was baptized into the Catholic Church, and sympathized with her difficult, disorderly later years. It was in Claude's defense that Colette once wrote: *"Ne divaguè pas glorieusement qui veut* . . . Not all those who wish to can go astray gloriously." In 1931, Claude published a sketch of

Colette's life and personality which is slightly gauche but wonderfully rich in *choses vues* and anecdotes: "One day Colette and her publisher were discussing a contract she had just signed, and the publisher said, 'But come, Colette, you do love money, don't you?' At which Colette snapped back, 'It horrifies me. And it's precisely because I loathe it so that I want to keep as much of it as possible locked up in my drawer.'"

🌷 Colette and Souci on the patio of La Treille Muscate.

In the spring of 1930, Colette published *Sido,* a triptych memoir of her parents, and a masterpiece. In July, she visited the fjords of Norway on the Rothschild yacht, and by August she was back in Saint-Tropez. "Despite precise and pressing commitments, I am doing *nothing* but making use of the good weather and my body, swimming, eating, sleeping, walking, even playing tennis . . . It's scandalous, of course, but nothing else suits me so well."

❦ Bel-Gazou at seventeen.

In 1931, a second film version of *La vagabonde* was made, and the assistant director was Bel-Gazou—no longer a schoolgirl, but Mlle Colette de Jouvenel, *"mystère et beauté"* (Claude Chauvière).

❀ Colette with La Chatte and Souci.

Winter brought bronchitis, and the doctor advised sunlight, adding, "I think you've played around with this Palais-Royal cave long enough." So by February 1931 Colette had installed her books and furniture at 74, Champs-Elysées, in two adjoining rooms with twin balconies on the sixth floor of the Hôtel Claridge. To the left, she could see the Place de la Concorde; to the right, the Arc de Triomphe. At night, she could look down on nocturnal birds passing over the glitter of traffic lights. On her balconies, whose wrought-iron railings she garnished with chicken wire for the safety of Souci and La Chatte, she grew geraniums and strawberries in pots. One day, La Chatte found a tree frog; on another, Colette herself saw a squirrel. "The fauna of Paris hotels is still little known."

In March 1931, *Vu,* a French weekly, published pictures of Colette, Anna de Noailles, and Marie Laurencin, with the heading: "The three most celebrated women in France."

🌷 Colette, self-portrait

🌷 La Comtesse Mathieu de Noailles, self-portrait.
A French-born Rumanian, Anna de Noailles (1876–1933) was the author of romantic novels and somewhat alabaster poetry (*Le coeur innombrable*), as well as one of the great monologuists of the Paris literary salons of the early twentieth century. Colette and she were friends, and at her death Colette was elected to her chair in l'Académie Royale de Langue et Littérature Françaises de Belgique. For years she received visitors in bed, and "one morning she let her tiny hands fall and exclaimed, 'Try to make me understand how one can live without love!' "

❧ Marie Laurencin, self-portrait.

Painter of pastel-pretty *jeunes filles en fleur,* Marie Laurencin (1885–1956) also designed stage sets for Diaghilev—notably for Poulenc's elusively lesbian ballet *Les biches*—and was the mistress of Apollinaire, to whom Picasso introduced her in 1908. She and Colette were never close, though they moved in contiguous circles, and around 1930, Marie gave Colette an oil painting of a young girl. There is an extensive portrait of her bold charm and abrasive wit in the *Journals* of Marcel Jouhandeau, who records that, "as she lay dying, Marie asked that a picture of her mother and her letters from Apollinaire be sealed in her coffin."

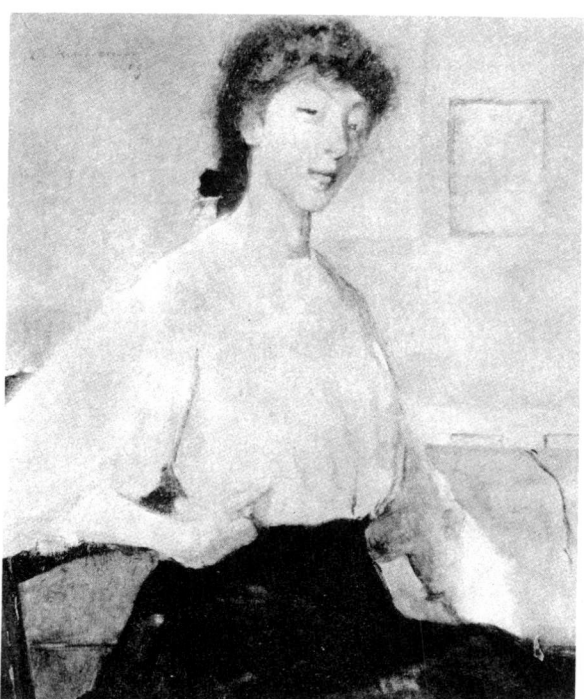

✿ Colette at her desk in La Treille Muscate. (Etching by Dunoyer de Segonzac.)

The summer of 1931, as usual, was spent at Saint-Tropez, working on a book of autobiographical essays for which she had not yet found the right title but whose substance, complex and controversial, she later described as "my personal contribution to the general repository of knowledge on the various forms of sensuality." Then on September 6, still in Saint-Tropez, she stepped into a ditch and broke the fibula of her left leg. It seemed a fairly minor accident at the time and healed readily through the autumn, but later it was suspected to have been the origin of her arthritis.

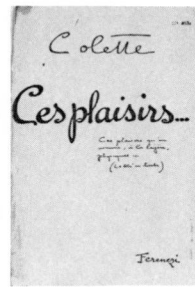

🌸 The original cover of *Ces plaisirs* . . . , as designed by Colette, with the epigraph in her own handwriting.

This was the "study of sexual inversion" Colette told Proust she had been unable to write. Her renewed attempt to do so may have originated in a brief memoir of Renée Vivien published privately in 1928 (and included in *Ces plaisirs* . . . as Chapter 5). In any case, she worked on the text for nearly two years, completing it on November 5, 1931. "Unfortunately," she complained, "the publisher will write on the title page: 'A Novel.' But it will not be a real novel." In fact, the publisher did no such thing, for the book amounts to nine autobiographical essays, aphoristic and anecdotal, on the nature of the senses, on sexual variety and anomaly, on homosexuality in men and women, on jealousy, on what the motto taken from *Le blé en herbe* called "those pleasures which are frivolously called physical."

"It will be a very moral book," she told an interviewer, but when the text was serialized in *Gringoire,* a weekly magazine, the reader reaction was so hostile that the editor cut off the fourth installment in the middle of a sentence and inserted "The End." Colette was shaken.

🌸 Slightly revised, and with a frontispiece by Jean Cocteau, *Ces plaisirs* . . . was reprinted in 1941, during the German Occupation, with a new and definitive title, *Le pur et l'impur*. "It will perhaps be recognized one day that this was my best book."

❦ In the early months of 1932, Colette suffered from an obstinate, brutal attack of shingles—psychosomatic, perhaps, and certainly related to the painful reception of *Ces plaisirs* . . . But at the same time she was preparing to launch her next project, an explicitly, even aggressively, nonliterary one.

❦ Again and again, Colette had expressed her distaste for writing. Now, with the worldwide Depression in its third year, she decided that she must have a second métier. Backed by a group of stockholders that included the Pasha of Marrakesh and the American-born Princesse Edmond de Polignac, she began to manufacture and market a line of beauty products under her own celebrated name, with a sleekly modern salon on the rue de Miromesnil and a Tout-Paris opening on June 2, 1932.

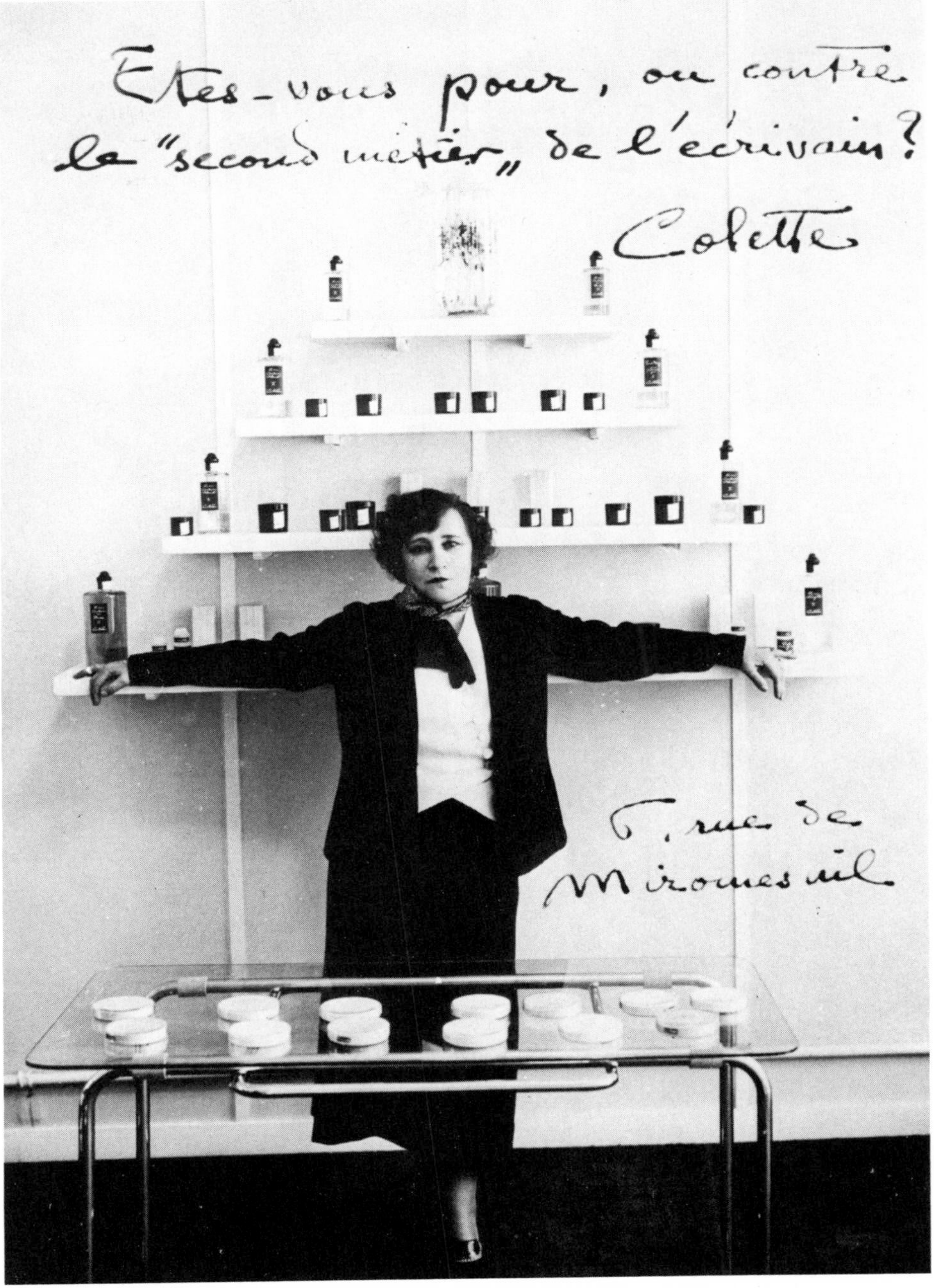

Êtes-vous pour, ou contre
le "second métier" de l'écrivain?

Colette

7 rue de
Miromesnil

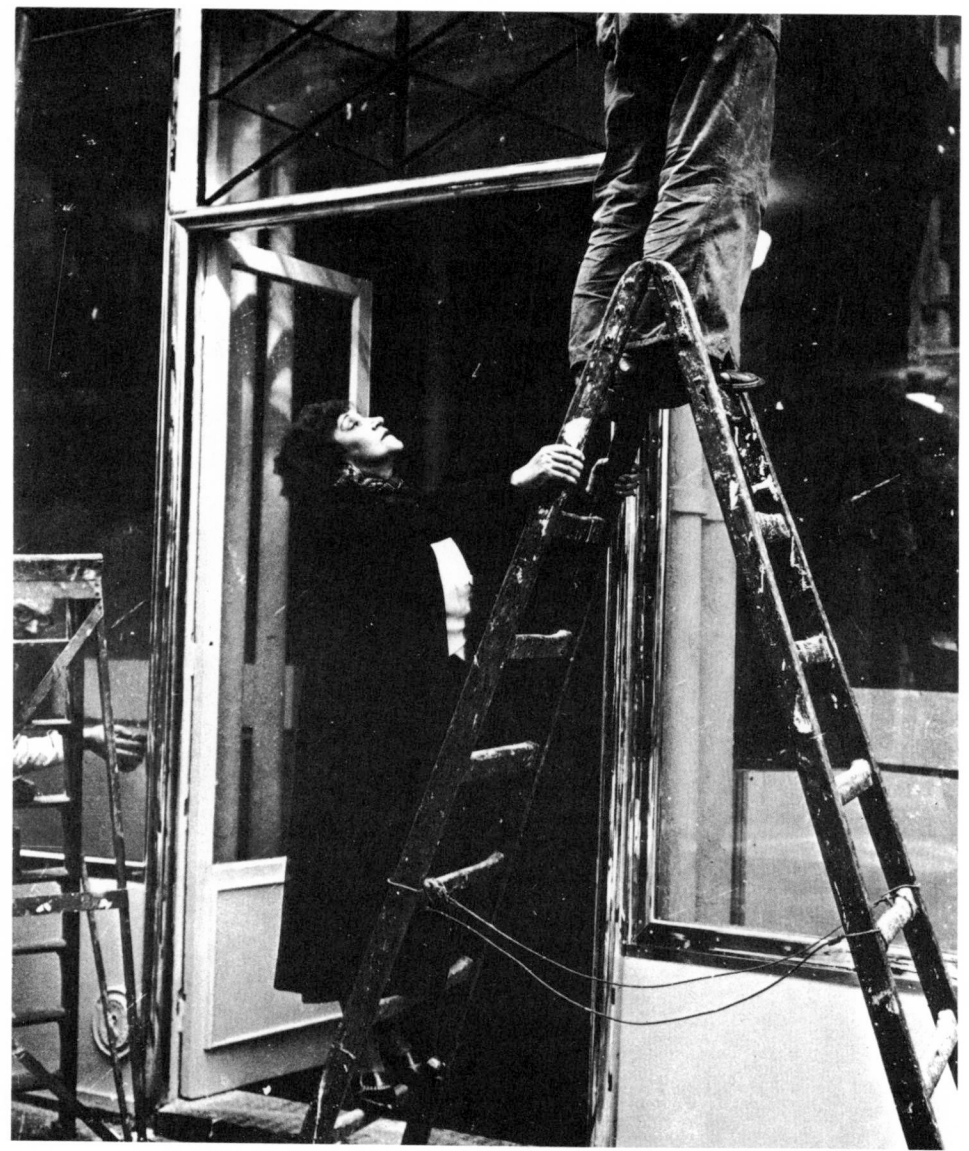

❦ Colette giving last-minute instructions to a workman outside her shop

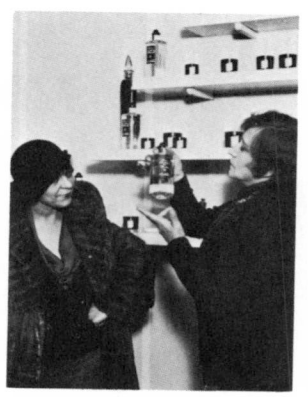

🌷 Colette with Hélène Jourdan-Morhange. "My new beauty-shop life as a maker of face-paintings would amuse you."

🌷 Colette making up actress Cécile Sorel, who, said Natalie Clifford Barney, "wanted to help publicize the enterprise. But Colette changed her method from one eye to the other, and the result was an asymmetry which doubled the great actress's age and discouraged other volunteers."

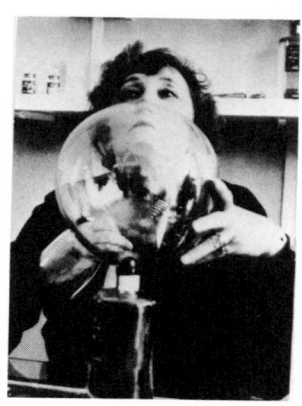

🌷 What was left of the year was dispersed in personal appearances throughout France, with a second shop opening in Saint-Tropez. Eventually, other projects, literary and cinematic, evolved, and by 1933 the Salon de Beauté had quietly come to an end.

Colette with one of her Guardian Angels.
"La Chatte dernière," the last of Colette's cats, who shared her household with the bulldog Souci, loved "a very pretty American popular song called *My Blue Heaven,*" and served as the model for Saha in *La Chatte,* the novel with Colette's most original plot, in which a young bride competes with her husband's pet cat for his love . . . and loses. "La Chatte" died in February 1939, just four weeks before Souci, and Colette's way of showing her love for them was to eschew all successors. "Our perfect companions never have fewer than four feet."

La Chatte was published in July 1933, and on the cover of its Bastille Day issue *Annales* featured Colette's pensive, kohl-eyed photograph. Doubtless, it was as a result of this kind of publicity that she was asked in August to become drama critic for *Le Journal*. "I realize," she wrote Hélène Picard, "that I have to return to journalism, however briefly." She held the post for the next five years.

❧ Colette with the tiny black opera glasses (*la jumelle noire*), "lucid to the point of being a little cruel," with which she scrutinized the stage. Her weekend reviews appeared from October 8, 1933, through June 5, 1938, and encompassed everyone and everything on the Paris stage, from Cocteau and Claudel, Sacha Guitry and her beloved Marguerite Moreno, to Noël Coward and García Lorca. She wrote, always, as someone who had herself appeared behind the footlights. About the author of *As You Like It,* she said: "Shakespeare worked without knowing he would become Shakespeare"—as penetrating a view of the Bard as any ever printed. Her columns were eagerly read, much quoted, and collected yearly into volumes called *La jumelle noire I, II, III, IV*. The final volume, interrupted by the outbreak of World War II, was included in her 1949 *Oeuvres complètes*.

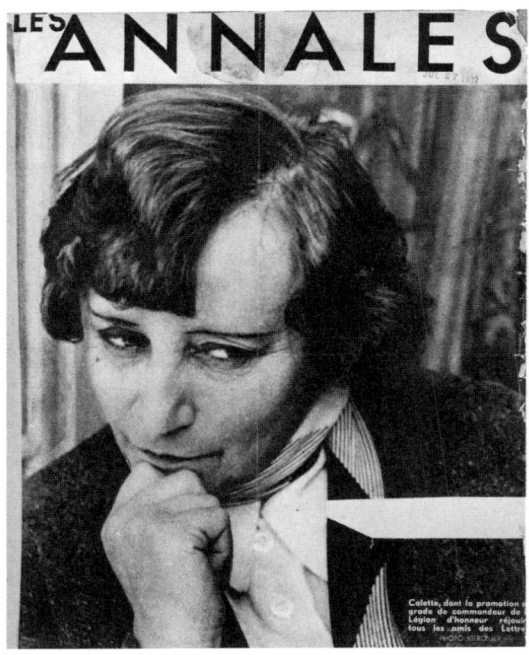

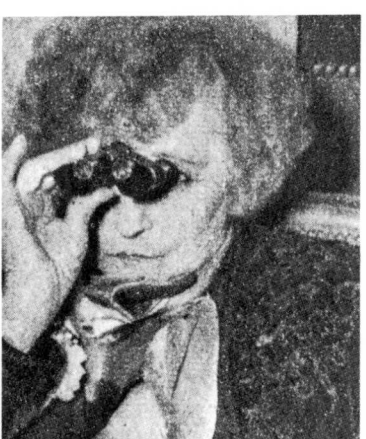

❦ Rehearsing a scene from *Lac-aux-dames,* a 1934 film for which Colette wrote the dialogue. Left to right: Simone Simon, Jean-Pierre Aumont, and Gide's protégé, director Marc Allegret.

Producer Philippe de Rothschild has described working with Colette: "To get the dialogue down on paper, I had to 'go to bed' with her. Now be careful. I mean nothing dubious. Colette used to do her writing in bed, with a little table on her knees. I would sit beside her bed and say, Now this is what the characters must say. It's a love scene. She thinks this, he thinks that. And Colette would suggest two or three inspired lines of dialogue, which she would then write down in her marvelous handwriting."

The film's male lead, playing a character not unlike the hero of *Le blé en herbe,* was Jean-Pierre Aumont. One summer day, when the heat was stifling, he visited Saint-Tropez to introduce himself to Colette. He found her watering her garden. "Take off your clothes," she said, and sensibly hosed him down.

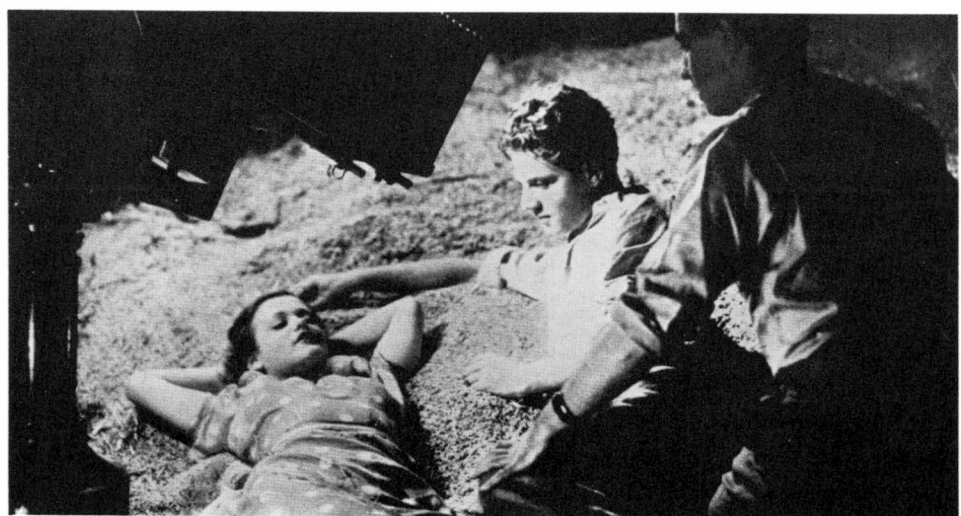

❦ A scene from *Divine,* for which Colette wrote her only original screen scenario, based on the backstage atmosphere evoked in her *L'envers du music-hall* sketches of 1913. The film was directed by Max Ophüls, and the screen credits named Bel-Gazou as co-adaptor. In this scene, a young dancer is nursing her child in the wings, *echt* Colette. There was also a characteristic moment in which the star, Simone Berriau, had a live python draped about her shoulders. Otherwise, the script was not very subtle, contrasting the artificiality and corruption of life backstage to the wholesome fresh air of life on a farm. The hero was a pretty milkman, the heroine a country girl seduced by the glamour of big-city lights: Claudine, as it were, over again, in the simplistic terms of popular moviemaking in the thirties.

🌷 Colette with Souci, sandals, foulard, and self-assured stride.

In spite of beauty salons, film scenarios, and a weekly column that necessitated her spending several evenings a week in a theater, Colette continued to write novels. In November 1934, *Duo* appeared, a short, terse account of a wife who has an affair and a husband whom it drives to suicide. "There is no jealousy that is not physical," she told Frédéric Lefèvre. "Anyone who honestly believes the contrary is mistaken."

On the morning of April 3, 1935, ten years after they met, Colette and Maurice Goudeket were married in the 8th arrondissement of Paris and Colette signed the license with a name none of her worldwide admirers would have recognized: Gabrielle Goudeket. With their witnesses, the newlyweds then proceeded to an inn called "Au père Léopold," in the Chevreuse Valley, about forty kilometers southwest of Paris, where they dined on *omelette à la crème* and ham knuckles. On the way back home (it was Wednesday, and Colette had four plays, including one with her old comrade Polaire, to review for her weekend column), there was a brief, unseasonable snowfall. Maurice stopped the car, and Colette stepped out on the roadside to let the large, feathery flakes fall on her uplifted face.

❦ Maurice Goudeket. "A man does not love a woman for her genius: he loves her in spite of her genius."

🌸 Madame and Monsieur Maurice Goudeket, on the Observation Deck of New York City's Empire State Building.

In early June 1935, the *Normandie,* France's newest Atlantic passenger ship, made its maiden voyage to New York. Colette and Maurice went along as special reporters, and they visited Woolworth's ten-cent stores, which Colette adored; the Parker pen factory, where she stocked up on her favorite *stylos;* and the Roxy Theater, where they ogled Mae West in her latest film. On the way back to their hotel, they encountered a stray cat. *"Enfin,"* cried Colette, "finally someone who speaks French!"

🌸 Colette, photographed in her room on the twenty-fourth floor of the Waldorf-Astoria Hotel by George Platt Lynes.

Glenway Wescott met Colette at a cocktail party given by her American publishers: "I remember her strong hands—serious writing is a manual labor! —and her fine feet in sandals, perhaps larger than most, rather like the feet of Greek goddesses. I remember her slightly frizzly hair fetched forward almost to her eyebrows, because . . . she has a square boyish or mannish forehead. I remember her delicate nostrils and her painted thin lips."

When the *Normandie* made its return voyage three days after its arrival, Colette and Maurice were on board, homesick already. "Oh, the taste for France . . . That prickling in the eyes when you hear someone say, 'You can see the coast . . .' The truth is, France has a savor which nothing else can quite match."

❧ Bel-Gazou, at twenty-two, with her father and her bridegroom.
August: "My daughter is getting married. I don't know the date yet, but I've had a very pretty letter from Jouvenel thanking me for permitting her to be married in Corrèze."
October: "My daughter was married last August 11. She is getting a divorce. Irrefutable reason: physical horror. One doesn't argue with that."

❧ Henry de Jouvenel, Senator and High Commissioner of the French Republic in Syria.

At only fifty-nine years of age, Henry de Jouvenel suffered an embolism while coming out of the Paris Automobile Show on the evening of October 5, 1935, and died later that night. He was buried at Castel-Novel. "I had not seen Henry de Jouvenel for twelve years," Colette wrote to Hélène Picard, "and I probably would not have recognized him on the street. Before his recent photograph, it seems that I said, *'Ah! Il est perdu.'* I believe his wife's grief must be very great."

🌷 Monsieur Willy had died in 1931, and in the interim a book about their marriage had slowly been germinating. Published in early 1936, it was called *Mes apprentissages: Ce que Claudine n'a pas dit*—with the notorious trade name again evoked to entice readers at the height of the Depression. For there were always money problems. Though she had been promoted to the order of Commandeur in the Légion d'Honneur in January, that same month she and Maurice were translating an American play (George S. Kaufman and Edna Ferber's *The Royal Family*), and in February, at sixty-three, she returned to the music-hall stage for four weeks of reminiscing and singing Burgundian folk songs.

❧ André Gide read *Mes apprentissages* "with a very lively interest. There is much more than mere talent here: a very particularly feminine sort of genius and a great intelligence. What choice, what ordering, what happy proportions in a narrative so apparently casual! What perfect tact and courteous discretion in the revelation of other people's secrets . . . There is not a word which does not count." Then, being Gide, he primly added: "I skirted the circles Colette is describing here, and against which an unconscious remnant of Puritanism happily put me on guard. In spite of her superiority, it does not seem to me that Colette was not somewhat contaminated."

🌷 Colette's sandal-shod feet, with the little bridge-like writing table she used while stretched full-length on her divan. Two anthologies of her writings, *Morceaux choisis* (selected by herself) and *Textes choisis* (selected by Pierre Clarac) came out in March, to mark her election to l'Académie Royale de Langue et Littéraire Françaises de Belgique.

❧ Elected to the Comtesse de Noailles's chair, Colette appeared
in person on April 4, 1936, to be officially welcomed and to read her own
Discours de réception. Though she had felt a genuine satisfaction at this honor
—especially since the Académie Française was, and still is, open to men only—
she had been uneasy about preparing a suitable speech, and as the day approached, she suffered from an immoderate stagefright. "Nevertheless, when
she rose, very straight in a simple, floor-length, black dress, her voice was
firm, her hands did not tremble a bit, and she gave a model reading."

❧ Colette thanks the poet Valère Gille, who has just presented her
to her peers. "The only virtue on which I pride myself," she said, "is my
self-doubt. If every day I find myself more circumspect toward my work, and
more uncertain as to whether I should continue, my only assurance comes
from my fear itself. For when a writer loses his self-doubt, the time has come
to lay aside his pen."

🌼 Colette, by Vertès.

In the spring of 1937, Colette experimented with a new medium. The Paris Radio engaged her to give a series of weekly talks, discussing whatever she wished, which, of course, meant her mother, cats, raising children, *l'art de vivre*. "I believe that there are more urgent and honorable occupations than that incomparable waste of time we call suffering."

🌼 Colette as a faun. (Lithograph by Luc-Albert Moreau.)

There were always interviewers. In March 1937, one of them asked Colette for her definition of *le bonheur*. "Happiness," she replied, "is a question of changing your troubles . . . Happiness is to be found in a certain form of anxiety, even in material hardship, rather than in serenity . . . Action is necessary to happiness. How many people do we see retiring to live on their pensions who then perish of boredom?"

Colette, from an etching by Jean Cocteau.

Colette and Jean Cocteau had been friends since the early twenties, and in the thirties she reviewed two of his plays, *La machine infernale* and *Les Chevaliers de la Table Ronde,* praising his "unique privilege . . . of intimate phantasmagoria." Cocteau, in turn, "asked Colette one day how it happened that, with her immense talent, she had not yet written what one could call a large-scale work. She stood me in front of a mirror and said: 'Look at yourself. I want to live, I want to have a solid body and decent legs. But look at you. You don't even have a behind to sit down on!' "

Colette at La Treille Muscate, summer 1937.
In ten years, Saint-Tropez had changed from a quiet fishing port to a chic watering hole, its quais lined with yachts, expensive boutiques, and noisy tourists. One season, Colette even discovered that there was a postcard depicting her "Villa." She forbade its sale and bought up the vendor's remaining supply for 150 francs. In 1939, La Treille Muscate was sold.

❦ Colette under the Académie Française's Coupole, where she was the first woman ever to be received—not as a member, but as a guest—on November 23, 1937. The event made waves all the way across the Atlantic, where America's *Life* magazine ran Colette's picture and improbably quoted her as saying she wrote "as easily as frying an egg."

The same day saw the publication of *Bella-vista,* a novella and three short stories, which brought some harsh reviews. The title story, vulnerably told in Colette's own first person, was about two seemingly lesbian innkeepers, one of whom turns out to be a man hiding out from the law. A reviewer named Charles Bourdon accused Colette of "unwholesome seduction . . . One feels her living in this atmosphere of immorality . . . like a worm in the mud." By Christmas Eve, she was depressed. "Books are selling badly. What we need is a desert isle."

🌸 Renée Hamon, during her 1937 voyage to the South Seas; and in 1942. A boyish, "rough, and well-scrubbed" native of Brittany, Renée Hamon (1897–1943) first met Colette in the late twenties, but their friendship did not ripen until ten years later, by which time Colette had nicknamed her Le Petit Corsaire. Born to wanderlust, Renée bicycled around the world in 1933–36 and in 1937 visited Tahiti and made a film about Gauguin's last years. On her return to Paris, she wrote an account of her adventures, called *Aux îles de la lumière,* which Colette encouraged, prefaced, and warmly promoted. Her premature death from cancer during the German Occupation is poignantly recorded in *Lettres au Petit Corsaire.* The week she died, Colette described her, in a letter to Marguerite Moreno, as "my little comrade-confrere-protégé."

🌼 The Palais-Royal gardens, from Colette's windows.

In January 1938, Colette moved into the *piano nobile* of 9, rue de Beaujolais, an apartment in the historic quadrangle of the Palais-Royal for which she had been waiting over ten years. Her three tall windows faced south and overlooked tidy flower beds, a vigorous fountain, and strolling neighbors, who would look up and greet her as she leaned on her windowsill. At night, it was almost as quiet as it had been in Saint-Sauveur. "Forty-five years have not changed me . . . I am still a country girl looking for her lost province in the twenty arrondissements and two riverbanks of Paris."

❧ Colette with a neighbor under the Palais-Royal arcades.
"I am working with perfect humility. In the past fortnight, apart from my
Paris-Soir pieces, I have written a publicity text for a tobacco company, the
preface for an enchanting new edition of Redouté's flower paintings, corrected
the proofs of *Le toutounier,* and dispatched several other odd jobs which help
to keep my stove warm." Colette had given up her theater column in 1938 and
had promptly gone to work as a "special reporter" for *Paris-Soir*. It is no won-
der, with such an agenda of commitments, that *Le toutounier* (a sequel to
Duo) was barely 30,000 words long. Its neologistic title referred to an over-
sized bed in the studio apartment shared by three sisters.

🌺 Colette at her writing table

"My instinct is and always has been to flee the symbol, which inspires nothing in me."

"When I'm commissioned to write something, I take the number of sheets of paper I'll need, and when I see the pile they make, I tell myself, 'You're going to have to cover all those pages!' "

"You should never use the word *indescribable*. Since a writer's job is precisely to describe, the word *indescribable* does not belong in his vocabulary."

❦ War broke out September 1. A few days before, Colette had been in Dieppe: "What beautiful weather! Almost as beautiful as in 1914!" But she returned to the Palais-Royal at once. "There is no question of my leaving Paris. My eyesight is poor, and consequently I don't see clearly from a distance." She began to broadcast overseas for Paris Mondial, describing daily life and morale in the City of Light. "Paris has never been more beautiful. Emptied, in part, of its civilian population, it looks much larger. It is recovering the harmonious proportions of an uncongested city. The scale of its squares is easily visible.

Very old arteries, ordinarily filled with commercial traffic, become narrow by-ways again, destined for pedestrians. An ancient building finds itself surrounded once more by the space its architect originally planned . . . In the nighttime quiet, Paris again hears sounds it has forgotten, the bells of the Angelus and the early Mass; and, before daybreak, the hoarse bellowing of a river barge crosses a vast silence of water and gardens and colonnades, of the Seine and the Tuileries, the Louvre, the Carrousel, and the Palais-Royal, to reach me in my sleep."

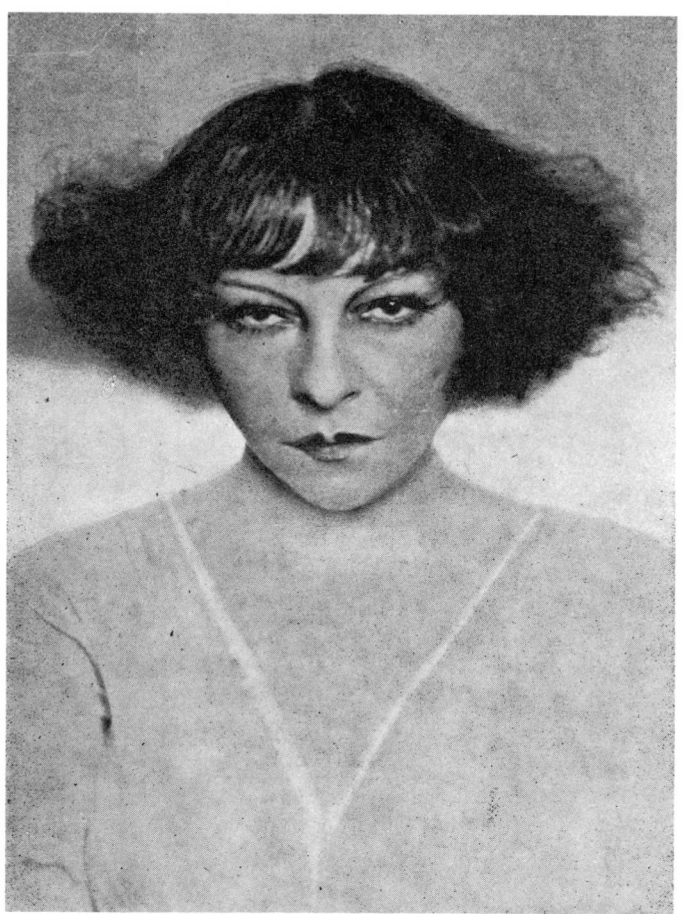

🌷 Polaire.

On October 11, "on one of those days of black rain which bring tears to the

eyes," Polaire died. "Twilight, winter, rain were never easy for her. I remember that when she was young, beautiful, shining, successful, the end of the afternoon was enough to plunge her into gloom."

✥ Colette, May 1940.

At the end of the winter of the "phony war," Colette spent a week in Nice, and while she was walking on the Promenade des Anglais, her purse was stolen. The local papers picked up the story, and two days later Colette received a note saying, "I didn't know it was you," and enclosing 3,000 francs. In Paris, a cynical newspaper observed that Madame Colette certainly had imagination and knew better than anyone else how to manage her own publicity.

By May, she was installed in a weekend house she had bought in a suburb called Méré. There was a large garden and the nightingales were profuse. Then, on June 3, Paris was bombarded for the first time. At four o'clock on the morning of June 12, Colette, Maurice, and their housekeeper, Pauline, packed their car and joined the mass exodus, heading south, away from the Germans and toward Corrèze, where Bel-Gazou's country house offered refuge.

Curemonte was a snug, safe place for a sixty-seven-year-old lady of letters to sit out the war, or so one would have thought. There were no food shortages, no occupying soldiers, no anxieties over a husband who was Jewish. But Colette became restless from the moment she arrived. After four weeks, she was almost indignant. "I wanted to stay in Paris, and now, in spite of everything, I am sorry I didn't. In this all-green tomb called Curemonte we have spent a month without mail, telephones, gasoline, or newspapers. We might have won the war and not know it. It's much harder to endure than danger." She kept writing, first an account of her flight from Paris, then a short novel, *La lune de pluie;* and finally she obtained enough black-market gasoline to get to Lyons and then start back north. "I am used to spending my wars in Paris," she was quoted as saying.

❧ She was back at her Palais-Royal window on September 11, and by October she had begun a weekly column on Paris life under the Occupation, full of practical advice about eating, keeping warm, caring for children. Here, too, she expressed her devotion for her fallen France: "Like many Frenchmen, comfort-loving and cranky, but capable of long admiration for what pleases them, I feel for my country a love that is rooted in my deepest being . . . And it is with this love as with all love: joy teaches us little about it. We take it for granted when we are happy. We are sure of its presence and its strength only when we are in pain."

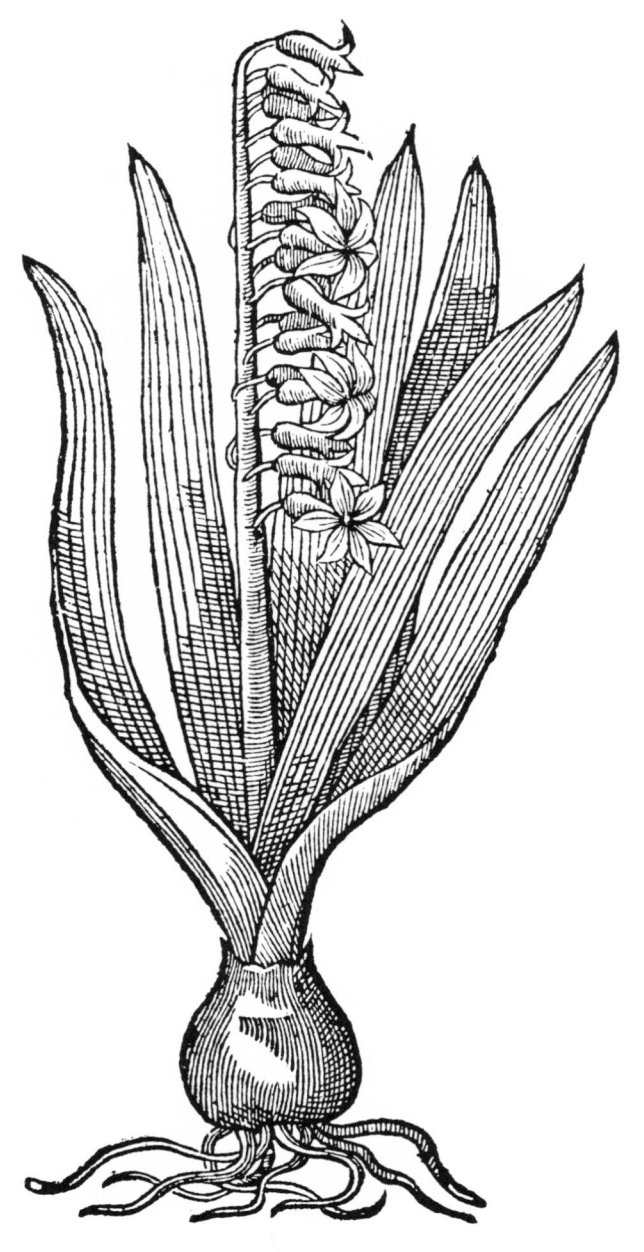

De Ma Fenêtre

La journée penche vers le soir.

Evening is almost here.

COLETTE, *L'étoile vesper*

❧   Almost five years were to pass before Colette left the precincts of Paris again. At first she got around on a bicycle, until a pain in her left hip, diagnosed as arthritis, began to trouble her and presently made even walking difficult. Meantime, there were many friends, life from her window, and the making of books. In the fall of 1940 came *Chambre d'hôtel,* another short, tart novel about an unsavory husband, his sickly wife, and a treacherous mistress; and again Colette told the story herself, diplomatically guiding the sheltered reader through unconventional moral terrain. The winter of 1940–41 was fierce. From her window, Colette described passers-by exclaiming about the cold—*"Il fait froid!"*—with the two successive *f*'s making graphic puffs of breath on the frosty air. Against the misery of unheated rooms, she counseled staying in bed. But spring finally came, and her column for March 20 reported the arrival of a honeybee. Mail had also been reestablished between Paris and the Unoccupied Zone, and Colette received imaginatively practical tokens from Bel-Gazou: "My daughter writes on the shells of a dozen eggs she sends me from Corrèze: twelve love letters and a tiny portrait of herself."

❧ Jean Cocteau was now a neighbor on the rue de Montpensier side of the Palais-Royal quadrangle, and he and Colette often took the air together. Ever fertile, he was writing a new play, *La machine à écrire,* about blackmail in the provinces under Nazi dominion, and Colette described him at work in front of his arched window under the arcades, "with his tuft of fuzzy hair, his greyhound leanness, and his sleeves rolled back to reveal hands like vine branches."

❧   La Princesse Edmond de Polignac, born Winifred Singer of the American sewing-machine family, was perhaps the greatest patron of music in the twentieth century, having commissioned scores from Fauré and Stravinsky, from de Falla and Poulenc. Maurice Goudeket has described her as "cold, timid, and intimidating . . . but for her air of a millionaire orphan and for the lucid humor with which she looked at herself in private, Colette had adopted her." They were close friends for years, and La Princesse "would climb Colette's stairs to drink mulled wine or share a debauch of cheese as if she were going to a grand party."

❦ Though their respective temperaments and *oeuvres* could hardly have been less alike, Colette and Paul Valéry (1871–1945) had at least two qualities in common: each earned his living on the open market as a professional writer, and each brought a highly polished and humbly conscientious quality of workmanship to his literary product. They met now and then, on juries or committees, or at the same luncheon, and it was on one of the latter occasions, as guests of Dr. Henri Mondor, a surgeon (he had removed Bel-Gazou's appendix), a bibliophile, and an authority on Mallarmé, that Valéry suddenly collapsed. As he was stretched out on a couch, Colette looked on "without any apparent compassion . . . 'Overworked writers don't understand,' she declared to her neighbor, 'but I do. From time to time, the harness must come off and the horse must be pastured out for a few days.'" Less than three years later, Valéry, still overworked, died.

❧ Francis Poulenc (1899–1963), a member of the Groupe des Six, composed chamber music, concert music (including a two-piano concerto commissioned by the Princesse de Polignac), operas, and over one hundred and fifty art songs to texts by Apollinaire, Cocteau, Eluard, Aragon, Jacob, Louise de Vilmorin, and Colette. "For years she used to promise me poems. Then one day when I was sitting with her on her divan-bed, I complained, and she said, 'Hold on, take this!' and laughing, she tossed me a huge gauze handkerchief on which was reproduced, in holograph facsimile, a pretty poem called 'Le portrait.' "

Poulenc's ballet *Animaux modèles,* based on La Fontaine's fables, was produced during the Occupation, and Colette reviewed both the music and its maker: "A big, bony boy, rural and gay, Poulenc lives in a large airy house surrounded by vineyards, and makes and drinks his own wine. Listen to his spangled instrumentation, see its golden, bubbly gleam! Look at Poulenc himself: is that the face of a water drinker?"

❦ Early in the morning of December 12, 1941, two German soldiers appeared at the door and arrested Maurice. Colette: "He left very calmly, charged with the crime of being a Jew." Maurice: "Colette accompanied me to the foot of the stairs. We looked at each other. Both smiling, we exchanged a rapid kiss. 'Don't worry,' I said, 'everything will be all right.' She gave me a friendly tap on the shoulder and said, 'Go.'"

By the twenty-first, Colette had discovered that Maurice was being held at a camp near Compiègne. "All communication is *impossible*. I'm waiting." Two days later: "Thirty-six men to a barrack room. Straw on the floor to

sleep on. Food not as bad as one would have thought. I wait. It's the hardest thing to do."

This continued for nearly two months, during which time Colette did everything to get Maurice liberated. "There was not a step she was not prepared to take, not a humiliation she was not prepared to face. She saw collaborators, she saw Germans. Who will blame her?"

Then, on the morning of February 6, 1942, Goudeket was suddenly, inexplicably, released. "For the moment," said Colette, "I am awarding myself the luxury of being very tired."

❦ "Where to moor yourself? To your work, I know that very well. But I also know that there are certain hours when one doesn't even have an anchor to drop into the unknown depths."

Despite her arthritic hip, black-market prices, and daily anxiety about Maurice's possible re-arrest, Colette's work record under the Occupation was prodigious. The weekly column went on, as well as other bits of journalism—a publicity text for D'Orsay perfumes one day, the preface to an exhibition of nineteenth-century décor the next. Then there were deluxe editions of shorter texts—*Noces, Mes cahiers, De la patte à l'aile, Flore et pomone, Broderie ancienne, Trois . . . six . . . neuf*, etc. There was a semi-*roman à clef* called *Julie de Carneilhan,* with a heroine whose initials reversed those of Colette when she was Madame de Jouvenel. There were several short stories; a tart novelette about the true course of sexual love, callèd *Le képi;* and a selection of columns called *Paris de ma fenêtre . . .*

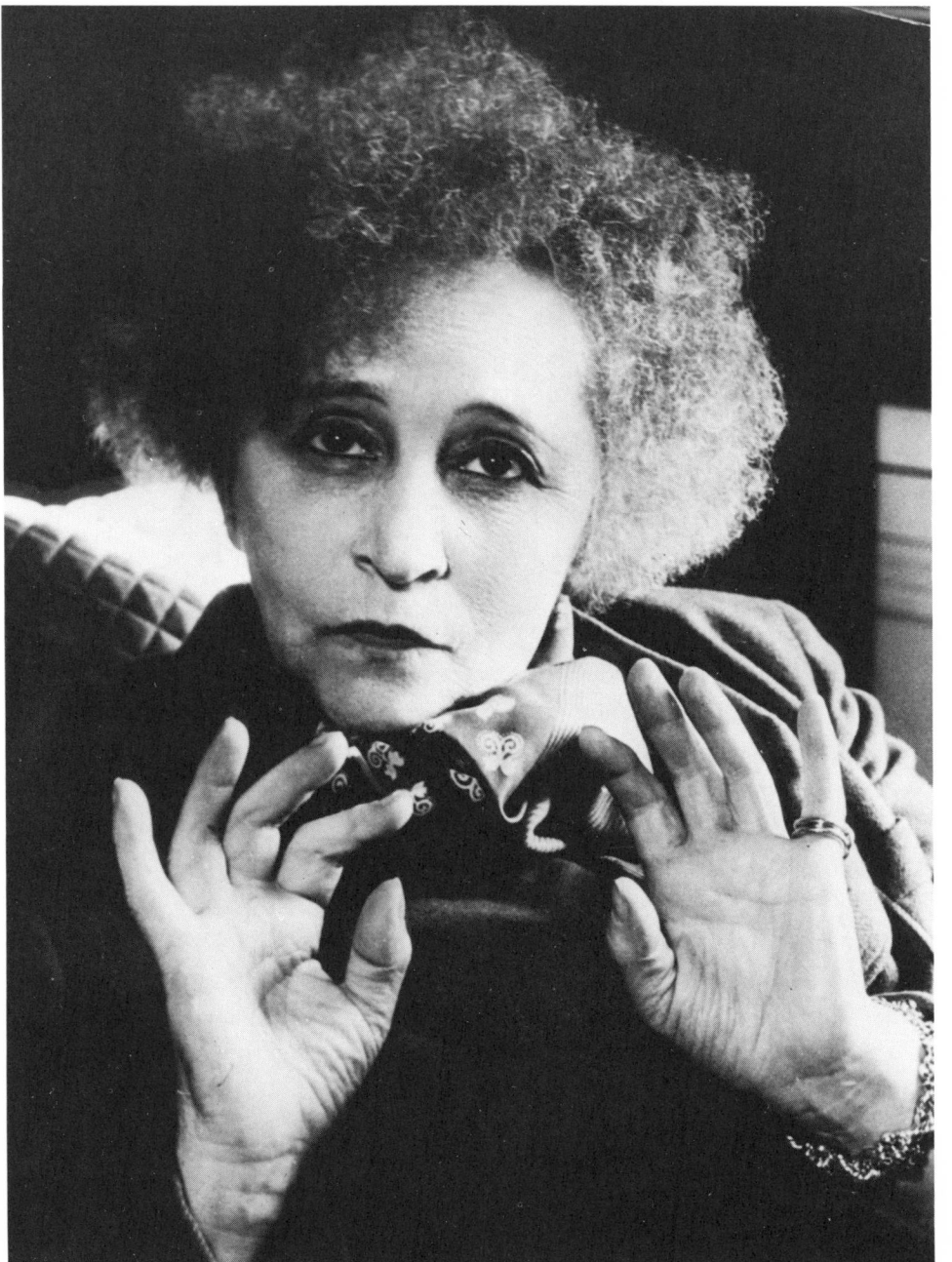

❧ There was also an astringently tender little fairy tale called *Gigi,* which Colette finished in the late summer of 1942 and which was first published in an obscure periodical in Unoccupied France and then in a limited Swiss edition before its perfect, improbably happy ending captured the Western world's heart in the spring of 1945.

❧ In August 1944—after "fifteen hundred days, as many days as it takes for a child to be born, grow, speak, and become an intelligent and ravishing human being"—came the Liberation of Paris. The war was not yet over in Europe, but on the night of the twenty-fourth, "tiny, handmade, ill-dyed tricolor flags fluttered like leaves from every window along the rue Vivienne. I could see no farther, because of my leg. But to the east a gleam indicated the Hôtel de Ville, its lights, its crowd, its armies, the new color of the soldiers' uniforms . . . That night came up like a dawn."

In late January 1945, Colette had news that Hélène Picard, whom she had not seen for three years, lay in a hospital, dying. A neighbor, Madame Marguerite d'Escola, called a few days later to bring details. "Colette received me on her couch, where her arthritis held her fast. There was a scarf knotted about her neck, and her eyes devoured my face as I spoke of the dying Hélène. We were in the hardest days of food rationing. A bar of chocolate lay on the table. Colette seized it and bit it in half with her solid teeth. 'Take her this piece from me!' The next day Hélène was dead."

On May 2, scarcely a week before V-E Day, Colette was unanimously elected to a chair in the Académie Goncourt. At the celebrating luncheon, she "posed her frizzled, felt-hatted, gray head and pointed her sandaled, red-toe-nailed feet" for photographers. Asked about her future plans, she replied, "I would like to love a little . . . to have flowers and strawberries . . . to live in a more tranquil universe."

❧ Colette at a Goncourt luncheon at Drouant's restaurant, hoisting her glass with co-Academicians Philippe Hériat and Armand Salacrou. "For all my playing the role of an old bachelor, I take a very feminine pleasure in finding myself the only woman surrounded by a tribunal of men."

❧ In the summer of 1945, Colette saw Provence again. She spent several weeks as the guest of Simone Berriau, working on a volume of memoirs to be called *L'étoile vesper,* and enjoying the company of Jean-Paul Sartre and Christian Bérard.

Cecil Beaton

🌷 Colette was never camera-shy, but from now on, as her celebrity grew not only in France but in Europe and America, she was photographed as frequently as a film star. British chronicler Cecil Beaton caught her in one of her least studied moments, though what she was saying remains unrecorded. Perhaps it was the same thing she said apropos a biography of Verlaine by her old friend Francis Carco: "Biographers tend to think it is easy to be a 'monster.' It's just as difficult as being a saint."

🌼   Though barely able to walk, Colette attended the opening night, in December 1945, of Jean Giraudoux's posthumous play, *La folle de Chaillot,* with Marguerite Moreno in the title role. She admired Bérard's décor and savored Moreno's performance with "its audacious coquetries of a plumed horse," but she "did not feel passionately about the text," and quoted Marguerite as saying that her role "was without secrets and involved no human mystery"—Colette's own view, more or less, of Giraudoux's entire *oeuvre*. The play, nevertheless, turned out to be Moreno's greatest, and last, triumph. She played it on and off over the next three years, until her "brusque and shattering effacement" came, after a brief touch of pleurisy, on Bastille Day, 1948.

🌢 Life became more and more restricted, but, on the other hand, along with a constant stream of visitors, there were always Bel-Gazou, ever faithful Pauline, and Maurice (pronounced "Mau-r-r-rice," with a rolling Burgundian *r*). "Everything about art is monstrous," said Jean Cocteau, "and Madame Colette did not escape this rule. Monsters must have keepers or they devour us, and Maurice Goudeket was always the keeper of his wife's monsters." Which was perhaps why, beginning with *L'étoile vesper*, Colette began to refer publicly to her husband as *"mon meilleur ami."*

Lee Miller

🌷 Colette with Cocteau.
"I learned to respect Jean Cocteau before coming to love him. In those days, whenever I felt lazy, I would consider the example of this young man whose works are not frivolous yet who always works as though for the fun of it."

🌷 *"J'ai toujours mes visiteurs du soir* . . . I always have my evening visitors." They included Truman Capote, to whom Colette gave a crystal paperweight containing a white rose; Jean Genet, who stole nothing, behaved very decorously, and discussed vocabulary; photographer Gisèle Freund, for whom Colette had posed ten years earlier ("I was a passionate woman then"); and novelist Julien Green: "She has the most beautiful woman's eyes I know, as beautiful as an animal's, brimming with soul and sadness." There was also an imaginative Swiss publisher named Mermod, who proposed that every few weeks he send her some flowers, whatever happened to be seasonal or appealed to him. In return, if she felt moved, Colette would write a page or two about whatever the flowers suggested to her. Time passed, flowers arrived—lilies, roses, orchids, anemones, poppies, hyacinths—and then in 1948 there was a charming book, *Pour un herbier,* containing twenty-two sketches, personal, reminiscent, anecdotal, of the floral kingdom.

When novelist-diarist Marcel Jouhandeau called on Colette in 1949, he recalled his earliest encounter with her in 1924, at the opening of a theater in the Place Danton. A young, little-known writer, he stood talking during an intermission with the eminent publisher Gaston Gallimard. Colette came up behind him, and as he was leaning on his cane, she gave it a brisk kick and nearly sent him sprawling. "Since Colette had no idea who I was, this malice on her part attracted me to her. Everyone has his own way of offering you his attention."

Now they discussed Jouhandeau's pet pigeons and their passion for hempseeds. "I'm sure they do love hempseeds," cried Colette, "but what you don't realize is that it is a vice on their part . . . When I was a little girl and we went out to play in the fields, my mother never failed to remind us not to lie down near hemp plants, because they would put us to sleep. Dear, wise Sido, how had she observed this, she who was certainly unaware of the fact that hempseeds are a species of hashish?"

In December, Gide received a letter written on blue paper: "If I were André Gide, I'd visit Colette." And a few days later, the eighty-year-old diarist did just that. But "the meeting lacked spontaneity . . . Neither party had much to say to the other," wrote Jean Lambert, Gide's son-in-law. "When we talked to Gide about it the next day, he had thought Colette a little too 'bitten' by the taste for publicity: he reproached her for being constantly 'on stage.'" Yet her prose never failed to delight him. Reading *Bella-vista,* he found the language "almost excessively savory . . . How Colette's way of writing pleases me! What assurance in her choice of words! What a delicate feeling for nuance! *'I seated myself very sulkily before a piece of writing begun without eagerness, abandoned without decision.'* Now it is this *'abandoned without decision'*—discreet to the point of passing unnoticed by most readers—which ravishes me."

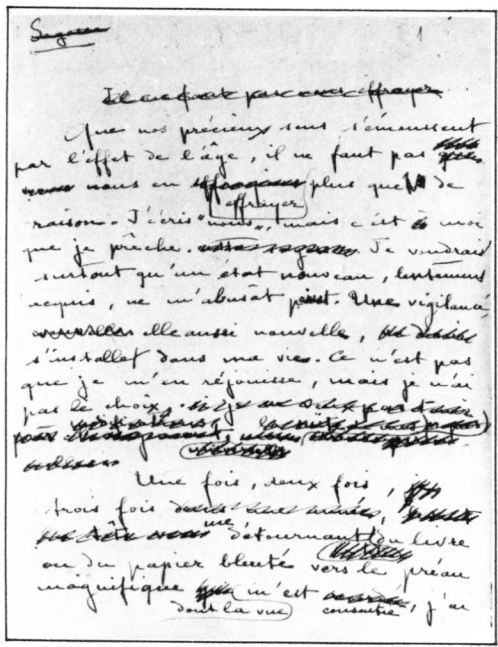

❧ Holograph of the opening page of *Le fanal bleu.*
A sequel to *L'étoile vesper,* this was Colette's last book. (Later titles, *En pays connu, Belles saisons, Paysages et portraits,* are collections of earlier texts.) The title came from Colette's work lamp, which she habitually shaded with a piece of her blue writing paper and which anyone strolling in the arcades at night could see gleaming like a river beacon to mark safe passage. Relaxed now, with no deadlines in particular, Colette wrote as she pleased, of weather and vineyards and children and herself growing older; above all, of her fellow human being as a creature "who does not escape his bodily envelope and who betrays it at a very high price."

ŒUVRES COMPLÈTES
DE

COLETTE
de l'Académie Goncourt

VI

CHÉRI
LA FIN DE CHÉRI
LE VOYAGE ÉGOÏSTE
AVENTURES QUOTIDIENNES

Le Fleuron
se vend à Paris, 26, rue Racine, chez
FLAMMARION

🌸 Late in 1949, the first of fifteen stately volumes of Colette's collected writings, "established under the author's eyes through the good offices of Maurice Goudeket," began to appear. The imprint on the title page was Colette's own, Le Fleuron, and the colophon flower was based on one of her sketches. The whole was printed on laid paper, in red as well as black ink, with a bibliography, and sold for 21,000 francs. In her tiny general preface, Colette declared that she had not ventured to rewrite. These volumes "retain all the marks of time, of error, of haste. Fresh on one page, flawed farther on, may their blemishes bear witness to my age, my long laboring, and the honorable evolution which transforms a bold writer into a timorous critic."

✿ Colette as her readers saw her.

W. H. Auden:
I am reminded of only one other novelist—Tolstoy.

Louise Bogan:
She can be compared to little but herself because she has written her discoveries down just as she herself made them . . . This, we can conclude, is her only secret.

Emilio Cecchi:
In her absolute femininity, Colette is not only one of the happiest artists of our time but one of the wisest and most profound interpreters of the inner life.

Janet Flanner:
She was attached to nature in an adult intimacy unique in the literary civilization of France . . . Born with talent, she achieved style. She was a scrupulous worker who by a kind of *fétiche* always wrote on pale blue paper as if writing indoors on a patch of sky.

Somerset Maugham:
I think no one in France now writes more admirably than Colette, and such is the ease of her expression that you cannot bring yourself to believe that she takes any trouble over it . . . I asked her. I was exceedingly surprised to hear that she wrote everything over and over again. She told me that she would often spend a whole morning working upon a single page.

Thierry Maulnier:
French literature has had to wait for Colette in order to have its Vergil and its Theocritus.

🌱 Colette presiding at a Goncourt lunch with (*standing*) Armand Salacrou, Philippe Hériat, André Billy, and (*seated*) Francis Carco: "I know Colette very well. I know that she is not tender, or, rather, that she has a horror of appearing so."

✿ In Monte Carlo, with Pauline, Maurice, and Prince Pierre of Monaco.

In the final lustrum of her life, Colette was virtually immobilized, a wheelchair being her only means of locomotion other than human arms. To distract her from her daily *douleur,* Maurice organized their winters in Monte Carlo. They came down from Paris by plane and for five successive seasons occupied the same ground-floor apartment in the Hôtel de Paris, "opening out onto a bit of garden and a more important wedge of the Mediterranean. While Maurice comes and goes, Pauline settles me in my wheelchair gadget against a sunny garden wall. Arthritis apart, I'm not to be pitied."

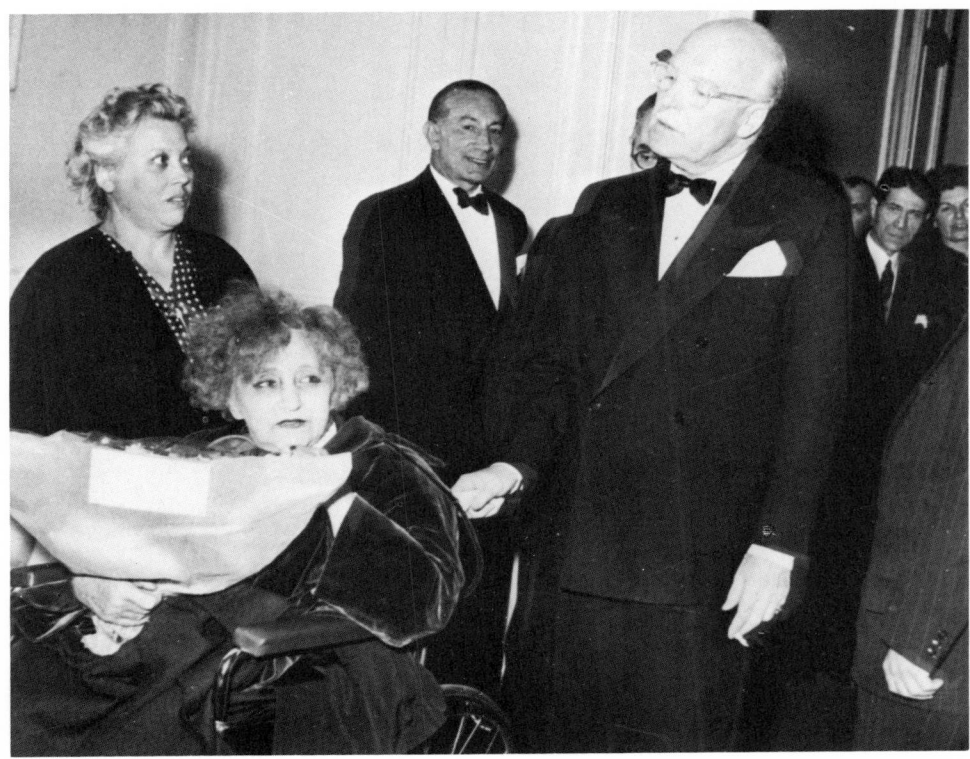

🌸 For a revival of *Chéri,* Colette revised the original script severely. The title role was played by Jean Marais, hero of Cocteau's films *La belle et la bête* and *L'éternal retour;* and veteran Boulevard star Valentine Tessier was his mothering mistress.

🌸 Colette with Audrey Hepburn, 1951.
The extraordinary destiny of the novella *Gigi* continued to unfold. There had already been a French film version when in 1951 the American author of *Gentlemen Prefer Blondes,* Anita Loos, adapted it for the New York stage. All that was needed was a French-looking young woman who could speak English and act. One afternoon, a film company was working on location in the lobby of the Hôtel de Paris. Colette passed by on her way to lunch and stopped to watch a British girl (Audrey Hepburn) performing in French, with a British accent. It was an epiphanic moment. Colette turned to Maurice and said, *"Voilà notre Gigi pour l'Amérique."* And so it was that, "at seventy-eight years of age, Colette, with a simple glance and the right word, caused a new star to rise in the theatrical firmament."

🌸 Colette with the cast and director of *Le blé en herbe.*
Not only *Gigi,* but several other novels of Colette's were brought to the screen in the early fifties: *Julie de Carneilhan, Minne, Chéri;* there was even an Italian version of *La Chatte.* The best was Claude Autant-Lara's adaptation of *Le blé en herbe,* with Edwige Feuillère as the Lady in White and a pair of newcomers, Michel Beck and Nicole Berger, as the young lovers.

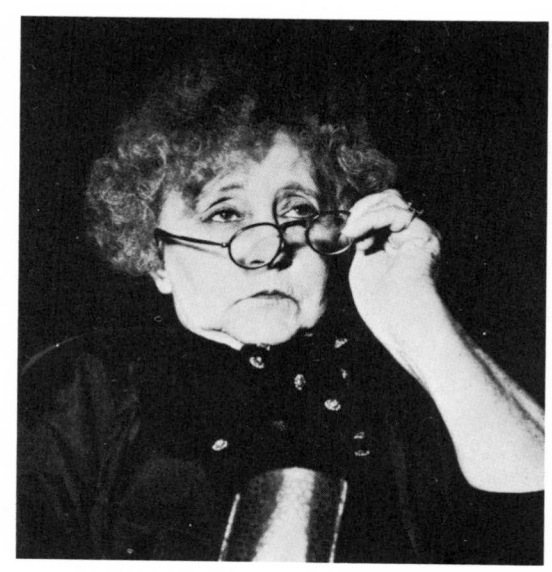

❦ Two views of Colette watching herself on the screen at the film's première, November 1952. "We never look enough, never exactly enough, never passionately enough."

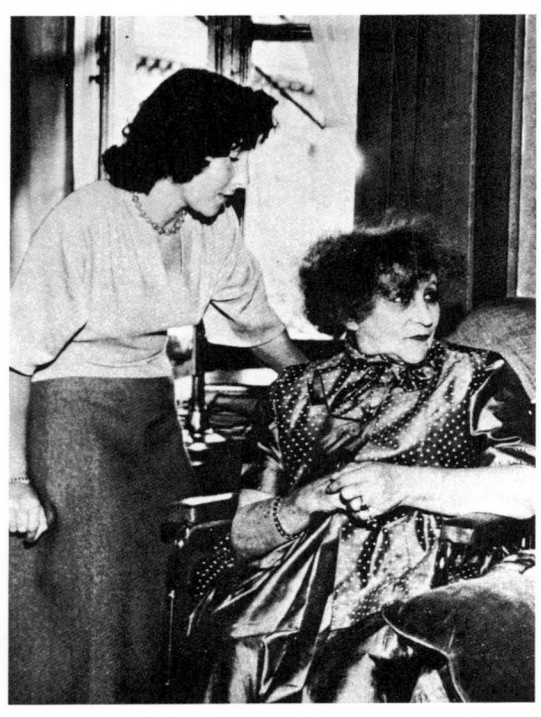

🌷 Colette with Yannick Bellon, watching a rush from the day's filming.

The most interesting Colette film, the one likeliest to be shown in one hundred years, is an intimate, non-commercial half hour directed by Yannick Bellon and called simply *Colette*. Made in the Palais-Royal apartment, it begins with Colette waking up, having her *petit déjeuner* with Maurice, and discussing the day's shopping with Pauline. It continues with a retrospective look at various of Colette's houses and concludes with a visit from Cocteau. Colette is visibly shy in some scenes, winningly pert in others—crunching an onion, stealing a strawberry—and in certain close-ups proves for all time that Maurice was right when he said: "There were no more beautiful eyes in the world, nor any which knew better how to see."

❦ Of the three windows facing the garden in the rue de Beaujolais apartment, two belonged to a larger room where Colette had worked and received for years, and the third to a smaller room, occupied by Maurice. Perhaps because she was born in a room "which it was never possible to keep adequately heated," Colette suffered all her life from any form of cold. Now, since it was easier to keep the smaller room toasty warm, Colette installed herself there, in what became known as *"la petite chambre rouge."* The walls were hung with

red silk, the curtains were red, the divan-bed was red, too. About her, Colette gathered her daily tools—a barometer, her *fanal bleu,* her collection of multi-colored paperweights, her writing table, her fur blanket, her fountain pens, her magnifying glass, her framed butterflies, her *pomologies,* and always a vase or two of fresh flowers. By special permission of the Palais-Royal Historical Committee, panes of glass were fitted into the lowest panels of her window, so she could watch as much of what was going on as possible.

🌺 *(left to right)* Maurice, Pierre Brisson, François Mauriac, Colette. In November 1952, when François Mauriac was awarded the Nobel Prize, one of the first things he did was to call on Colette, who should have had it, he felt, in his place.

🌺 For her eightieth birthday, on January 28, 1953, Colette was surprised *chez elle* by her co-immortals of the Académie Goncourt, who arrived bearing a specially prepared luncheon and cake, all courtesy of Drouant's restaurant. Bel-Gazou cut the cake; Gérard Bauër, Francis Carco, Alexandre Arnoux, Roland Dorgelès, André Billy, and Armand Salacrou looked on; and Colette herself blew out the token eight candles. "I cannot say that she ever took me into her confidence," Bauër has written. "Modesty, or perhaps her provincial origins, prevented this. So much so that when one of her admirers questions me . . . I can only reply, 'Read her books. She tells more about herself to those who read her than she ever told to those who knew her in person.' "

❦ Very old, very tired, very much cherished and honored, Colette was made a Grand Officier of the Légion d'Honneur in April 1953. The next month, from the hands of the American ambassador to France, she accepted honorary membership in the National Institute of Arts and Letters. One of her last manuscripts read: *"Tout ce que je veux . . . mais ce ne serait pas encore assez!* Everything I want . . . but even that would not be enough!"

❦ Colette and Maurice on the board-walk at Deauville, summer 1953. One of Colette's favorite stories was told her by the illustrator Dignimont and recorded in his memoirs by Francis Carco. "There was a certain butter-fly so rare that the collector took a plane to bring it back to Paris. As he was delivering it to a museum, a second butterfly, hidden under the cage, flew out and then came back to alight beside his traveling companion. It was the male, who had not been able to separate himself from his mate, whom he had comforted throughout the flight." It may have been those butter-flies, as well as herself and Maurice, that Colette had in mind when she wrote one of her last sentences: *Lui, il avait moi, et moi, j'avais lui* . . . He had me, and I had him."

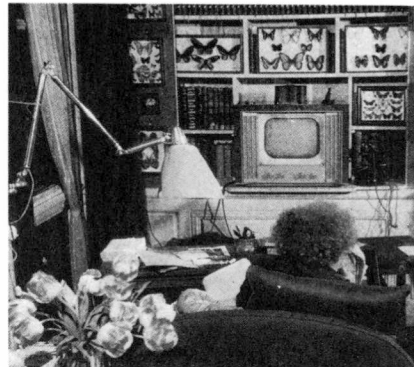

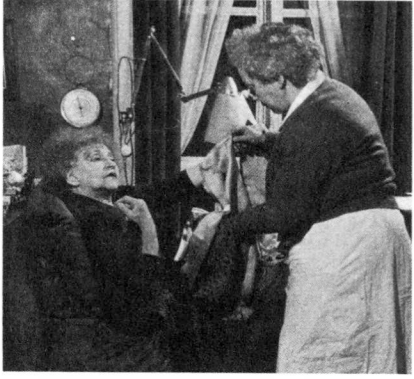

Paris-Match devoted the cover and a number of pages in its issue for March 13, 1954, to *"La fée du Palais-Royal."*

🌷 Colette at lunch: "I fear the presence of skeptics less and less . . . provided they furnish me with my daily ration of surprise. With a little pride, I can endure my pain. But I do need to be surprised. So take the trouble, please: astonish me. I do not know how to go on without these last bursts of laughter."

🌷 Colette on her divan: "Oh! how I'd like to feel the cold belly of a little frog on each hand."

🌷 Colette with Pauline: "Nothing human can console the melancholy of the chosen."

❧ Colette remembering: "Love has never been a question of age. I shall never be so old as to forget what love is."

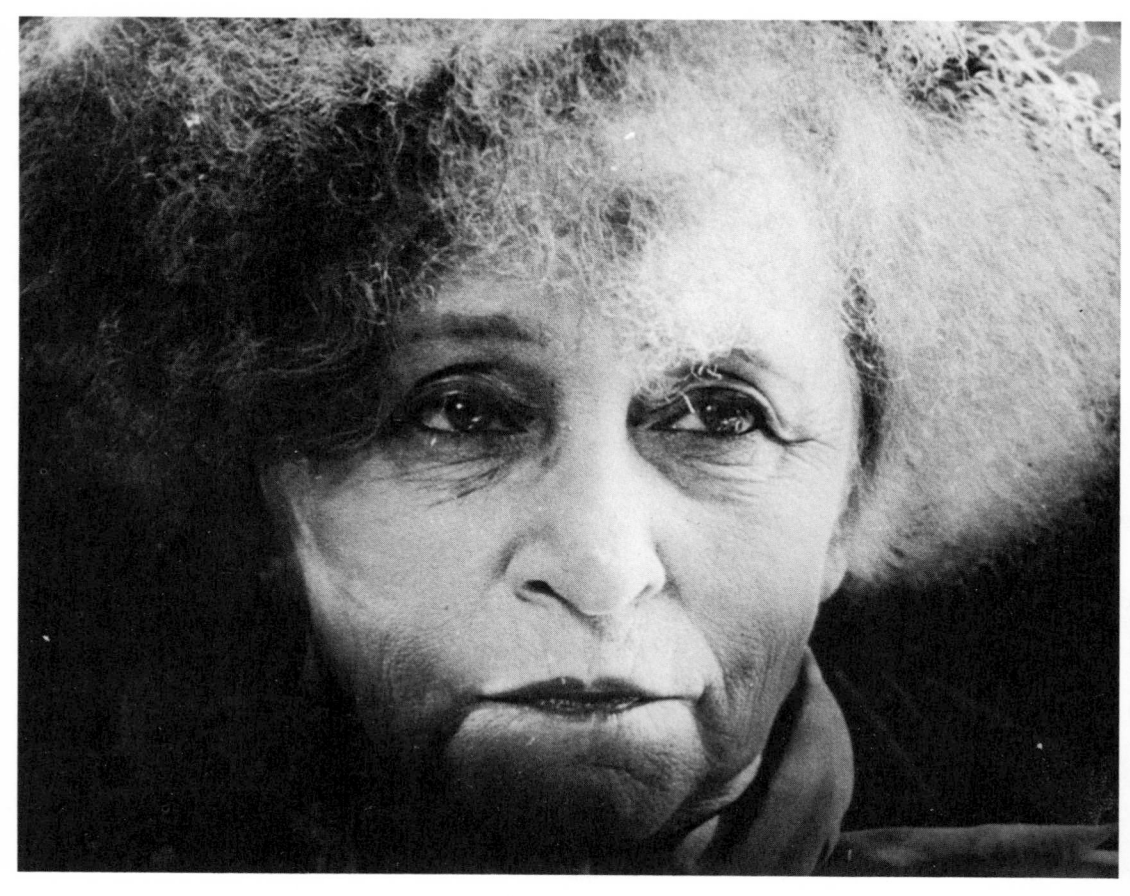

🌷   Colette, glimpsed in the diary of Renée Hamon, "Le Petit Corsaire":

A bourgeoise, an authentic bourgeoise (even in a hotel she has to "dress up" her room).

Feminine and yet so virile: a balance.

Her helpful humor. She is fraternal.

Strength. Health. Sanity: a sense of proportion, of *mesure*. Very French.

Courageous, original, loyal, enthusiastic, tender, tyrannical, epicurean.

Her professional honesty.

Alternately a cat, a panther, a ferret, a doe.

Her conversation: her mimicries—her petulance—her dynamism never cease to enchant me, to astonish me.

Unbelievably young: what draughts of pure oxygen one inhales in her presence!

Her eyes: for me they are blue, the blue of lapis—with the milky white of breast-fed children.

Eats her soft-boiled egg with cherries. Try it: it's exquisite.

A horror of "sham," or imitation.

Her age? What a joke! As if the date of one's birth were good for anything but an identity card or a passport.

Appendix

Colette: à vol d'oiseau

Notes and Sources

Bibliography

Colette: à vol d'oiseau

What a beautiful life. It's a pity I didn't notice it sooner.

COLETTE, *after seeing Yannick Bellon's film of her life*

1829   Colette's father, Jules-Joseph Colette (Le Capitaine), born in Toulon.

1835   Colette's mother, Adèle-Eugénie-Sidonie Colette (Sido), born in Paris.

1873   January 28: Sidonie-Gabrielle Colette born in Saint-Sauveur-en-Puisaye, Yonne, France.

> Gide is four years old, Proust and Valéry two. Rimbaud publishes *Une saison en enfer* at his own expense.

1889   Colette receives her *brevet élémentaire,* completing her formal education. Forty years later, her school principal remembered her ungratefully: "I am convinced that my ex-scourge was possessed by the soul of a cat."

1890   Public sale of Colette family's goods.

1893   May 15: married to Henri Gauthiers-Villars (Willy), settles on the Left Bank in Paris, at 28, rue Jacob.

1894   Mysteriously ill for several months.

1896   To Bayreuth for Wagner's *Ring* tetralogy.

1900   *Claudine à l'école:* signed by Willy alone.

> Oscar Wilde dies two blocks away. Puccini's *Tosca.*

1901   *Claudine à Paris.*

> Deaths of Queen Victoria and Toulouse-Lautrec. Kipling's *Kim.*

1902   *Claudine en ménage.*

> Death of Zola. Debussy's *Pelléas et Mélisande;* Gide's *L'immoraliste.*

1903   *Claudine s'en va.*

Gauguin dies in the South Pacific.
Gertrude Stein settles in Paris.

1904 *Dialogues de bêtes:* first book signed Colette Willy. *Minne.*

1905 *Les égarements de Minne.* Le Capitaine dies in September.

Les Fauves at the Salon d'Automne.
Jules Verne dies.

1906 Separation from Willy and alliance with the Marquise de Belboeuf (Missy). Debut as a mime.

Proust moves into his cork-lined room.

1907 *La retraite sentimentale.* Scandal at the Moulin Rouge provoked by an on-stage kiss with Missy.

Ravel's *Histoires naturelles* songs set to Jules Renard's texts.

1908 *Les vrilles de la vigne.*

Nietzsche's *Ecce Homo.*

1909 *L'ingénue libertine. En camarades* (play).

Gides's *La porte étroite.* Marinetti's *Manifesto of Futurism.* Gertrude Stein's *Three Lives.*

1910 *La vagabonde.* Colette meets Henry de Jouvenel and begins to write regularly for his newspaper, *Le Matin.*

Stravinsky's *L'oiseau de feu.* Mark Twain and Tolstoy die.

1911 Settles with Henry de Jouvenel at 57, rue Cortambert.

Nijinsky in *Spectre de la rose.* First Cubist pictures shown at the Salon d'Automne.

1912 Death of Sido in September, and marriage to Henry de Jouvenel on December 19.

Ravel's *Daphnis et Chloé.*

1913   *L'entrave. L'envers du music-hall. Prrou, Poucette et quelques autres.*
       July 3: birth of daughter Colette (Bel-Gazou).

                              Proust's *De côté de chez Swann.*
                              Duchamp's *Nude Descending a Stair-
                              case.* Apollinaire's *Alcoöls.* Mann's
                              Death in Venice.

1914   Henry de Jouvenel mobilized.

                              August 3: Germany declares war on
                              France.

1915   Colette in Rome and Venice as a special reporter.

                              Sarah Bernhardt's left leg amputated.
                              Death of Remy de Gourmont.

1916   *La paix chez les bêtes.*

                              Griffith's *Intolerance.* First Dadaist
                              exposition in Munich.

1917   *Les heures longues.*

                              Valéry's *La jeune parque.* November 7:
                              Russian Revolution.

1918   *Dans la foule.*

                              Deaths of Debussy and Apollinaire.
                              November 11: Armistice.

1919   *Mitsou.* Colette assumed editorship of *Le Matin*'s literary page.

                              Gide's *La symphonie pastorale.* Ravel's
                              Le tombeau de Couperin. Bauhaus
                              opens.

1920   *Chéri. La chambre éclairée.* Colette named Chevalier de la Légion
       d'Honneur.

                              Cocteau's *Le boeuf sur le toit.* Gide's *Si
                              le grain ne meurt.* Valéry's *Le cimetière
                              marin.*

1921   *Chéri* dramatized.

Pirandello's *Six Characters in Search of an Author*. García Lorca's *Book of Poems*.

1922   *La maison de Claudine*.

Death of Proust. Cocteau's *Le secret professionnel*. Hesse's *Siddhartha*.

1923   *Le blé en herbe*. Separation from Henry de Jouvenel. *La vagabonde* (play).

Freud's *The Ego and the Id*. Rilke's *Duino Elegies*.

1924   *La femme cachée. Aventures quotidiennes*.

Kafka and Conrad die. André Breton's *Manifeste du surréalisme*.

1925   Meets Maurice Goudeket. Tours with a company of *Chéri,* playing Léa. *L'enfant et les sortilèges* (opera libretto for Ravel's music).

Jules Renard's *Journal*. Kafka's *The Trial*. Chaplin's *The Gold Rush*.

1926   *La fin de Chéri*. Buys a house, La Treille Muscate, in Saint-Tropez. Tours the South of France playing the title role in *La vagabonde*.

Cocteau's *Orphée*. Gide's *Les faux-monnayeurs*. Babel's *Red Cavalry*.

1927   Moves into an apartment in the Palais-Royal.

Valéry received into the Académie Française. Brecht and Weill's opera *Mahagonny*. Death of Isadora Duncan.

1928   *La naissance du jour. Le voyage égoïste*.

Death of Thomas Hardy. Dreyer's *Passion de Jeanne d'Arc*. Gershwin's *An American in Paris*.

1929 *La seconde.*

> Joyce's *Ulysses* translated into French.
> Cocteau's *Les enfants terribles.*

1930 *Sido. Histoires pour Bel-Gazou.*

> Death of D. H. Lawrence. Robert
> Musil's *The Man without Qualities.*

1931 Moves to the top floor of the Hôtel Claridge on the Champs-Elysée.

> Boris Pasternak's *Safe Conduct.*
> Virginia Woolf's *The Waves.*

1932 *Ces plaisirs . . . Prisons et paradis.* Opens a Salon de Beauté on June 1.

> Hemingway's *Death in the Afternoon.*
> Cocteau's *Le sang d'un poète.*

1933 *La Chatte.* Begins a five-year stint as drama critic.

> Death of Constantine Cavafy. André
> Malraux's *La condition humaine.* May
> 13: 25,000 books burned outside the
> University of Berlin by the Nazis.

1934 *Duo. La jumelle noire.*

> Gertrude Stein and Alice B. Toklas tour
> America. August 2: Hitler assumes
> absolute dictatorship of Germany.

1935 *La jumelle noire II.* Married to Goudeket on April 3. Visits New York
in June. Henry de Jouvenel dies in October.

> Death of T. E. Lawrence (Lawrence of
> Arabia). Cocteau's *Portraits-souvenir.*
> T. S. Eliot's *Murder in the Cathedral.*

1936 *Mes apprentissages.* Received into the Académie Royale de Langue et
Littéraire Françaises de Belgique.

> Deaths of Kipling, Gorki, García
> Lorca. Gide's *Retour de l'U.R.S.S.*
> Chaplin's *Modern Times.*

1937 *Bella-vista. La jumelle noire III.*

Death of Ravel. Picasso's *Guernica.*
Jean Renoir's *La grande illusion.*

1938 *La jumelle noire IV.* Settles in the Palais-Royal for the second time, at 9, rue de Beaujolais.

Antonin Artaud's *Le théâtre et son double.* Sartre's *La nausée.* Marcel Jouhandeau's *Chroniques maritales.*

1939 *Le toutounier.*

Deaths of Yeats and Freud. Gide's *Journal 1889–1939.* Ernst Jünger's *On the Marble Cliffs.* Jean Renoir's *La règle du Jeu.* September 2: Great Britain declares war on the Third Reich.

1940 *Chambre d'hôtel.* Colette leaves Paris June 12, and returns to the Nazi-occupied city on September 11.

Deaths of Leon Trotsky and F. Scott Fitzgerald. George Orwell's *Inside the Whale.* Graham Greene's *The Power and the Glory.*

1941 *Journal à rebours. Julie de Carneilhan.* December 12: Maurice Goudeket arrested by the Germans.

Deaths of James Joyce, Virginia Woolf, and Isaac Babel. Bertolt Brecht's *Mother Courage.* Louis Aragon's *Le crève-coeur.*

1942 Goudeket liberated on February 6.

Albert Camus's *L'étranger.* Saint-John Perse's *Exil.*

1943 *Le képi. Nudité.* Colette begins to suffer acutely from arthritis of the left hip.

Sartre's *Les mouches*. Gide's *Interviews imaginaires*. Carl Dreyer's *Day of Wrath*.

1944 *Trois . . . six . . . neuf.*

Jean Genet's *Notre-Dame-des-Fleurs*. Alberto Moravia's *Agostino*. August 25: Liberation of Paris.

1945 *Gigi*. May 2: Colette is unanimously elected to the Académie Goncourt. August 15: end of World War II. Deaths of Valéry, Bartók, and Webern. Tennessee Williams's *The Glass Menagerie*. Sergei Eisenstein's *Ivan the Terrible*.

1946 *L'étoile vesper*. March–April: to Geneva for an arthritis cure. Death of Gertrude Stein. Cocteau's *La belle et la bête*. Carson McCullers's *The Member of the Wedding*.

1947 May–June: second arthritic cure in Geneva. Deaths of Bonnard and Whitehead. Jackson Pollock's first "Action" paintings. Camus's *La peste*.

1948 *Pour un herbier*. Death of Marguerite Moreno. Truman Capote's *Other Voices, Other Rooms*. Henry Green's *Concluding*.

1949 *Le fanal bleu. La fleur de l'âge. Oeuvres complètes,* in fifteen volumes, begins to appear. Jean Genet's *Journal du voleur*. Simone de Beauvoir's *Le deuxième sexe*. Nathalie Sarraute's *Portrait d'un inconnu*.

1950 *En pays connu.* Winters in Monte Carlo.

Deaths of George Orwell, Cesare Pavese, and G. B. Shaw. Marcel Jouhandeau's *L'imposteur.* Gottfried Benn's *Double Life.*

1951–54 Final years, bedridden and in constant pain, but still writing— *"C'est mon métier!"*—and immensely famous, her windows a Parisian landmark. She died the evening of August 3, 1954, "after a small sip of champagne" (Janet Flanner). Received a state funeral in the Cour d'Honneur of the Palais-Royal, and was buried under a pink granite tombstone in the Père-Lachaise Cemetery. Her posthumous books:

1955 *Belles saisons*

1958 *Chiens de Colette*
      Lettres à Hélène Picard
      Bêtes libres et prisonnières
      Paysages et portraits

1959 *Lettres à Marguerite Moreno*

1961 *Lettres de la vagabonde*

1963 *Lettres au Petit Corsaire*

1970 *Contes des mille et un matins*

1973 *Lettres à ses pairs*

1975 *Colette au cinéma*

Notes and Sources

EN PAYS CONNU ❦ 1954–73

SIDO ❦ 1873–93

MES APPRENTISSAGES ❦ 1893–1906

46 "Willy said to me . . ." Colette, *Mes apprentissages,* translated by Helen Beauclerk.

46 "odious piece of furniture . . ." Colette, *Mes apprentissages,* translated by Helen Beauclerk.

48 "At first . . ." Colette, *Mes apprentissages,* translated by Helen Beauclerk.

49 "The origin and anonymity . . ." Colette, *Mes apprentissages.*

49 "there will never be . . ." Quoted in *Colette* (Bibliothèque Nationale).

50 "I used Colette's . . . a marveling professor . . ." Letter from Willy to Rachilde, quoted in *Colette* (Bibilothèque Nationale).

51 "As far as I can see . . ." Sacha Guitry, quoted in *Colette* (Bibliothèque Nationale).

52 "I had this huge . . ." Letter from Colette to Rachilde, quoted in *Colette* (Bibliothèque Nationale).

52 "Their success . . ." Colette, *Oeuvres complètes,* Vol. I.

55 "voluble and full of beer . . ." Colette, *Mes apprentissages.*

55 "You wrote . . ." Colette, *Mes apprentissages.*

55 "I cannot like . . ." Colette, *Lettres à ses pairs.*

55 *"Willy ont beaucoup . . ."* Jules Renard, *Journal.*

55 "Claudine is a delicious . . ." Jules Renard, *Lettres inédites, 1883–1910.*

56 "You can't get away . . ." Colette, *Mes apprentissages.*

56 "What Polaire did . . ." Colette, *Mes apprentissages.*

59 "Your hair . . ." Colette, *Mes apprentissages.*

59 "Naturally, people . . ." Colette, *Lettres au Petit Corsaire.*

60 "Polaire! . . ." Jean Cocteau, *Portraits-souvenir,* translated by Richard Howard in *Professional Secrets.*

60 "A curious little animal . . ." Jules Renard, *Journal.*

61 "thirty or thereabouts . . . Ten years of Paris . . ." Colette, *Mes apprentissages.*

62 "At the beginning . . ." Natalie Clifford Barney, *Souvenirs indiscrets.*

63 " 'You look a bit green . . ." Colette, *Mes apprentissages.*

64 "delicious . . . adorable" Sido and Willy, quoted in *Colette* (Bibliothèque Nationale).

64 "Seriously speaking . . ." Preface by Francis Jammes to Colette, *Sept dialogues de bêtes.*

64 "a monk in the act . . ." Colette, from a letter to Francis Jammes, quoted in *Colette* (Bibliothèque Nationale).

67 "A prison is indeed . . ." Colette, *Mes apprentissages.*

68 "so young at seventy-six" Colette, in a letter to Natalie Clifford Barney, quoted in *Colette* (Bibliothèque Nationale).

68 "I never surprised . . ." Colette, *Sido.*

L'ENVERS DU MUSIC-HALL ❧ 1906–10

71 *"Les artistes . . ."* Colette, *La vagabonde.*

72 "from the highest . . ." Colette, *Ces plaisirs . . .*

72 "Bent over me . . ." Colette, *Les vrilles de la vigne.*

75 "dressed in . . ." Sylvain Bonmarriage, *Willy, Colette et moi.*

75 "fine wines . . . baronesses of the Empire . . ." Colette, *Ces plaisirs . . .*

75 "The lady of the house . . ." Colette, *Ces plaisirs . . .*

75 "Mathilde de Morny . . ." *Les albums de Colette: Naissance d'un écrivain.*

76 *"J'appartiens . . ."* Roger Peyrefitte, *L'exilé de Capri.*

76 "I had come . . ." Maurice Martin Du Gard, *Les mémorables.*

80 "The seduction . . ." Colette, *Ces plaisirs . . .*

83 "My husband . . ." Jean Chalon, *Portrait d'une séductrice.*

83 "Indiscretion is . . ." Natalie Clifford Barney, *Souvenirs indiscrets.*

83 *"C'est un chic type . . ."* Maurice Goudeket, *Près de Colette.*

84 "THE EX-MARQUISE . . ." Colette, *Lettres de la vagabonde.*

84 "You poor boob . . ." Colette, *La vagabonde.*

87 "It's frightful . . ." From a letter of Sido, quoted in Sylvain Bonmarriage, *Willy, Colette et moi.*

87 "I'm a little dismayed . . ." Jean Larnac, *Colette.*

88 "In a smugglers' cabin . . ." *Colette* (Bibliothèque Nationale).

LA FLEUR DE L'ÂGE ❦ 1910–25

123   "It seems . . ." Colette, *L'entrave.*

123   "It's fantastic . . ." Colette, *Lettres de la vagabond.*

124   "a new person . . ." Colette, *L'étoile vesper.*

124   "Whenever Sido . . ." Colette, *L'étoile vesper.*

127   "Musidora did . . ." Colette, *Le fanal bleu.*

128   "And the men here . . ." Colette, *"Journal intermittent: Notes d'Italie,"* in *Oeuvres complètes,* Vol. XIV.

129   "a delicious book." From *The Letters of Rainer Maria Rilke and Princess Marie Von Thurn und Taxis,* translated by Nora Wydenbruck.

130   "Whenever I come . . ." Colette, *La naissance du jour.*

130   "innocent of everything . . ." Colette, *"Bâ-Tou,"* in *La maison de Claudine.*

130   "The Eden permitted us . . ." Colette, *Le fanal bleu.*

133   "because she is . . ." Colette, "La Chienne Bull," in *La paix chez les bêtes.*

133   "I am not a crybaby . . ." Colette, *Lettres de la vagabonde.*

134   "She is spending . . ." Colette, *"Journal intermittent: 1941,"* in *Oeuvres complètes,* Vol. XIV.

135   "I wept a little . . ." Marcel Proust, as quoted in Claude Chauvière, *Colette.*

136   "If you would know . . ." Bertrand de Jouvenel, "Colette," in *Time and Tide,* August 14, 1954.

138   "bookish foster son" Bertrand de Jouvenel, "Colette," in *Time and Tide,* August 14, 1954.

138   "an imitation Musset . . ." Colette, *L'étoile vesper.*

138   *"carcoise"* Colette, *Lettres à ses pairs.*

138   "The most savory . . ." Francis Carco, *Rendez-vous avec moi-même.*

139   "sealed off . . ." Colette, *L'étoile vesper.*

139   "How can I ever . . ." Colette, *Paysages et portraits.*

140   "name derived . . . glossy as . . ." Colette, Preface to *Chéri* in *Oeuvres complètes,* Vol. VI.

140   "quasi-scrofulous . . ." Colette, quoted by Maurice Goudeket, *Colette et l'art d'écrire.*

140   "Madame, I have devoured . . ." André Gide, letter of December 11, 1920,

quoted in Claude Chauvière, *Colette*.

140   "I could not say . . ." Colette, *L'étoile vesper*.

143   "Sapène gave . . ." Colette, *Lettres à ses pairs*.

144   "She noticed me . . ." Maurice Martin Du Gard, *Les mémorables*, Vol. I.

145   "A life as pure . . ." Colette, *L'étoile vesper*.

147   "Houssard accused . . ." Colette, *Dans la foule*.

147   "I look in vain . . ." Colette, "Landru," in *Prisons et paradis*.

148   "She was called Pati . . ." Colette, *Bella-vista*.

151   "He writes his scenes . . ." Colette, in *Journal de Monaco*, December 9, 1924, quoted in *Colette* (Bibliothèque Nationale).

151   "When I was . . ." Colette, "Proust," in *Belles saisons*.

151   *"No one in the world . . ."* Colette, *Lettres à ses pairs*.

151   "Then one day . . ." Georges Simenon, *Portraits souvenirs: Entretiens avec Roger Stéphane*.

152   "Not without torment . . ." Colette, *Lettres à Marguerite Moreno*.

152   "But can't you . . ." Colette, *La naissance du jour*.

152   "Artisans, bureaucrats . . ." Quoted in Claude Chauvière, *Colette*.

152   "And so . . ." Colette, *La naissance du jour*.

155   "You cannot imagine . . ." Quoted by Lise Deharme, in *Les années perdues*.

155   "had left without" Colette, *Lettres de la vagabonde*.

156   "Ah! la, la . . ." Colette, *Lettres à Hélène Picard*.

156   "I'm accepting . . ." Colette, *Lettres à Marguerite Moreno*.

156   "it's terrible . . ." Colette, *Lettres à ses pairs*.

158   "I ski, I skate . . ." Colette, *Lettres à Hélène Picard*.

158   "I am never . . ." "Conversation with Colette," in *Living Age*, May 1931.

BELLES SAISONS 🌸 1925–40

161   *"Où ne s'est-elle pas fourrée . . ."* François Mauriac, quoted by Colette in *L'étoile vesper*.

162 "Someday . . . I told myself . . . Oh, Maurice . . ." Maurice Goudeket, *Près de Colette.*

165 "It's playing . . ." Quoted in *Colette* (Bibliothèque Nationale).

166 "In reality . . ." Gérard d'Houville, quoted in *Colette* (Bibliothèque Nationale).

166 "Is Colette . . . Let Madame Colette . . . the image of a Renoir . . ." Quoted in Jean Larnac, *Colette.*

168 "I was very . . . " Colette, "Vins," in *Prisons et paradis.*

168 "a difficult page . . ." Colette, *L'étoile vesper.*

168 "Into four liters . . ." Colette, "Trente-huit, cinq," in *Prisons et paradis.*

170 "When an older woman . . ." Colette, as quoted in Jean Larnac, *Colette.*

170 "hard, bitter . . . It was not a question . . ." Maurice Goudeket, *Près de Colette.*

171 "We have been living . . ." Colette, *Lettres à Hélène Picard.*

173 "handsome local boys . . . My father . . ." Colette, *Lettres à ses pairs.*

173 "excellent . . ." Colette, *Lettres au Petit Corsaire.*

174 "A modest rental . . ." Colette, *Trois . . . six . . . neuf.*

175 "vagabond indeed . . ." Natalie Clifford Barney, *Aventures de l'esprit.*

176 "irritation at . . ." Colette, *Lettres de la vagabonde.*

177 "Colette has always . . ." Paul Léautaud, *Journal littéraire.*

179 "To Colette . . . two admirable books . . ." François Mauriac, as quoted in Claude Chauvière, *Colette.*

179 "great classic writer" René Lalou, *Histoire de la littérature française contemporaine.*

179 "saying that . . ." Thornton Wilder, as quoted by Edmund Wilson, *The Shores of Light.*

181 "This is the nth time . . ." Colette, letter of January 1, 1928, quoted in *Colette* (Bibliothèque Nationale).

181 "One always writes . . ." Colette, *Lettres à ses pairs.*

182 "One day . . ." André Dunoyer de Segonzac, in a memoir in *Arts.*

182 "austere . . ." Colette, as quoted in an interview by Pierre Billotey, in *Annales,* December 1928.

182 "Why?" Maurice Goudeket, *Près de Colette.*

184 "She is now a short . . ." Janet Flanner, preface to *Mitsou, or How Girls Grow Wise.*

184 "As he arrived . . ." Julien Green, *Journal.*

184 "If we said to her . . ." Pierre Scize, as quoted in Claude Chauvière, *Colette.*

186 "One night . . ." Natalie Clifford Barney, *Souvenirs indiscrets.*

186 "I feel that if . . . that poor, infantile . . ." Colette, from a letter to Lady Una Troubridge, quoted in *Colette* (Bibliothèque Nationale).

186 *"Ne divaguè pas glorieusement . . ."* Colette, *Lettres à Hélène Picard.*

187 "One day Colette . . ." Claude Chauviére, *Colette.*

188 "Despite precise . . ." Colette, *Lettres à Hélène Picard.*

190 "I think you've played . . ." Colette, *Trois . . . six . . . neuf.*

190 "The fauna . . . " Colette, *Lettres à Hélène Picard.*

192 "The three . . ." Reported by René Gimpel, *Diary of an Art Dealer.*

192 "one morning . . ." Colette, *Lettres à Hélène Picard.*

193 "as she lay dying . . ." Marcel Jouhandeau, *Que la vie est une fête.*

194 "my personal contribution . . ." Colette, as quoted by Glenway Wescott, *Images of Truth.*

195 "study of sexual inversion" Colette, *Lettres à ses pairs.*

195–6 "Unfortunately, the publisher . . . It will be . . . it will perhaps be recognized . . . " Conversation with Colette," in *Living Age,* May 1931.

199 "My new beauty-shop . . ." Colette, *Lettres à ses pairs.*

199 "wanted to help . . ." Natalie Clifford Barney, *Souvenirs indiscrets.*

200 "a very pretty American . . ." Colette, *Le fanal bleu.*

200 "Our perfect companions . . ." Colette, *Lettres à ses pairs.*

200 "I realize . . ." Colette, *Lettres à Hélène Picard.*

201 "lucid to the point . . ." Colette, preface to *La jumelle noire,* in *Oeuvres complètes,* Vol. **X.**

201 "Shakespeare worked . . ." Colette, *La jumelle noire II.*

202 "To get the dialogue . . . Take off your clothes . . ." Philippe de Rothschild, as quoted from a 1973 television interview, in *Colette au cinéma,* by Alain and

Odette Virmaux.

204 "There is no . . ." Quoted from "An Hour with Colette," by Frédéric Lefèvre, in *Living Age,* February 1935.

207 "A man does not . . ." Maurice Goudeket, *Près de Colette.*

208 *"Enfin,* finally . . ." Maurice Goudeket, *Près de Colette.*

208 "I remember . . ." Glenway Wescott, "An Introduction to Colette," in *Images of Truth.*

208 "Oh, the taste . . ." Colette, *Lettres de la vagabonde.*

211 "My daughter is getting . . ." Colette, *Lettres de la vagabonde.*

211 "My daughter was married . . ." Colette, *Lettres à Hélène Picard.*

211 "I had not seen . . ." Colette, *Lettres à Hélène Picard.*

213 "with a very . . ." André Gide, *Journal: 1889–1939.*

215 "Nevertheless, when . . ." Maurice Goudeket, *Près de Colette.*

215 "The only virtue . . ." Colette, "Discours de réception," reprinted in *Belles saisons.*

216 'I believe that . . ." Colette, quoted in *Colette* (Bibliothèque Nationale).

216 "Happiness . . ." Colette, as quoted in interview in *Annales,* March 25, 1937.

217 "unique privilege . . ." Colette, review of *La machine infernale,* April 15, 1934, reprinted in *La jumelle noire.*

217 "asked Colette one day . . ." Jean Cocteau, as quoted by Claude Mauriac, in *Conversations avec André Gide.*

219 "as easily as frying . . ." *Life,* December 20, 1937.

219 "unwholesome seduction . . . Books are selling . . ." Colette, *Lettres au Petit Corsaire.*

220 "rough, and well-scrubbed . . . my little comrade . . ." Colette, *Lettres à Marguerite Moreno.*

222 "Forty-five years . . ." Colette, "Province de Paris," in *En pays connu.*

223 "I am working . . ." Colette, *Lettres à Hélène Picard.*

225 "My instinct is . . ." Colette, *Lettres à ses pairs.*

225 "When I'm commissioned . . ." Colette, *Lettres au Petit Corsaire.*

DE MA FENÊTRE ❦ 1940–54

246 "posed her frizzled . . . I would like to love . . ." Colette, as quoted in *Time* magazine, May 14, 1945.

248 "For all my playing . . ." Colette, *Le fanal bleu.*

249 "Biographers tend . . ." Colette, *Lettres à ses pairs.*

250 "its audacious coquetries . . . did not feel . . . was without secrets . . . brusque and shattering . . ." Colette, *Lettres à Marguerite Moreno.*

251 "Everything about art . . ." Jean Cocteau, *Poésie critique II.*

252 "I learned to respect . . ." Colette, in an issue of *Empreintes* (May 1950) devoted to Cocteau.

252 *"J'ai toujours mes visiteurs . . ."* Colette, *Le fanal bleu.*

252 "She has . . ." Julien Green, *Journal.*

254 "Since Colette . . . I'm sure . . ." Marcel Jouhandeau, *Carnets de l'écrivain.*

255 "If I were . . . the meeting lacked . . ." Jean Lambert, *Gide familier.*

255 "almost excessively . . ." André Gide, *Pages de journal, 1939–1942.*

257 "established under . . . retain all . . ." Colette, *Oeuvres complètes,* Vol. I.

258 "I am reminded . . ." W. H. Auden, *Griffin,* December 1951.

258 "She can be compared . . ." Louise Bogan, *A Poet's Alphabet.*

258 "In her absolute femininity . . ." Emilio Cecchi, *Aiuola di Francia.*

258 "She was attached . . ." Janet Flanner, Introduction to *Seven by Colette.*

258 "I think no one . . ." Somerset Maugham, *The Summing Up.*

258 "French literature . . ." Thierry Maulnier, *Introduction à Colette.*

260 "I know Colette . . ." Francis Carco, Preface to Colette's *Paris de ma fenêtre.*

261 "opening out . . ." Colette, *Lettres de la vagabonde.*

263 *"Voilà . . .* at seventy-eight . . ." Maurice Goudeket, *Près de Colette.*

264 "We never look . . ." Colette, *Paris de ma fenêtre*

265 "There were no . . ." Maurice Goudeket, *Près de Colette.*

266 "which it was never . . ." Colette, *Le fanal bleu.*

269 "I cannot say . . ." Gérard Bauër, "Le souvenir de Colette," in *Livres de France,* October 1954.

270 *"Tous ce que je veux . . ."* Holograph illustration, *Livres de France,* October 1954.

271 "There was a certain . . ." Francis Carco, *Rendez-vous avec moi-même*.

271 *"Lui, il avait moi* . . ." Colette, as quoted in Goudeket, *Près de Colette*.

272 "I fear . . ." Colette, *Paysages et portraits*.

272 "Oh! how I'd like . . ." Colette, *Le voyage égoïste*.

272 "Nothing human . . ." Colette, *Belles saisons*.

273 "Love has never . . ." Philippe Hériat, *Retour sur mes pas*.

275 "A bourgeoise . . ." from Renée Hamon's *Journal,* as quoted in Colette, *Lettres au Petit Corsaire*.

COLETTE: À VOL D'OISEAU

278 "What a beautiful life . . ." Comment by Colette to a journalist after seeing Yanick Bellon's film about her life, quoted by L. Maurice-Amour, in "Colette et ses musiciens," *Paris-Match*, September 1952.

Bibliography

Les albums de Colette: Naissance d'un écrivain. Geneva: Editions de Cremille, 1972.

Auden, W. H. "Colette," *Griffin* (New York), December 1951.

Barney, Natalie Clifford. *Aventures de l'ésprit.* Paris: Emile-Paul Frères, 1929.

———. *Souvenirs indiscrets.* Paris: Flammarion, 1960.

Bauër, Gérard. "Le souvenir de Colette," Paris: *Livres de France,* October 1954.

Bernac, Pierre. *Poulenc et ses poètes.* Pathé Marconi, Record Number CCA-1098.

Billotey, Pierre. Interview with Colette, *Annales,* December 1928.

Bogan, Louise. *A Poet's Alphabet.* New York: McGraw-Hill Book Company, 1970.

Bonmarriage, Sylvain. *Willy, Colette et moi.* Paris: Editions Charles Fremanger, 1954.

Carco, Francis. Preface to *Paris de ma fenêtre.* Geneva: Milieu du Monde, 1944.

———. *Rendez-vous avec moi-même.* Paris: Albin Michel, 1957.

Cecchi, Emilio. *Aiuola di Francia.* Milan: Mondadori, 1969.

Chalon, Jean. *Portrait d'une séductrice.* Paris: Stock, 1976.

Chauvière, Claude. *Colette.* Paris: Firmin-Didot, 1931.

Cocteau, Jean. *Portraits-souvenir.* Paris: Grasset, 1935.

———. *Colette.* Paris: Grasset, 1955.

———. *Professional Secrets.* New York: Farrar, Straus and Giroux, 1970.

Colette, *Oeuvres complètes.* Paris: Flammarion, 1949, 1973.

Colette. Paris: Bibliothèque Nationale, 1973.

Deharme, Lise. *Les années perdues.* Paris: Plon, 1961.

Dictionnaire biographique des auteurs, Vol. I.

Du Gard, Maurice Martin. *Les mémorables,* Vol. I. Paris: Flammarion, 1957.

Dunoyer de Segonzac, André. "Colette," *Arts, c.* 1958.

Flanner, Janet. Preface to English translation of *Mitsou, or How Girls Grow Wise.* New York: Albert & Charles Boni, 1930.

———. Preface to *Seven by Colette.* New York: Farrar, Straus and Cudahy, 1955.

Flanner, Janet (Genêt). "Letter from Paris," *The New Yorker,* August 21, 1954.

Gide, André. *Journal: 1889–1939.* Paris: Gallimard, 1939.

———. *Pages de Journal, 1939–1942.* New York: Pantheon Books, 1944.

———. "Hommage à Colette," *Le Point,* May 1951.

Gimpel, René. *Diary of an Art Dealer.* New York: Farrar, Straus and Giroux, 1966.

Goudeket, Maurice. *Près de Colette.* Paris: Flammarion, 1956. (*Close to Colette.* New York: Farrar, Straus and Giroux, 1957.)

———. *Colette et l'art d'écrire.* Annales de la Faculté des Lettres et Sciences Humaines d'Aix, 1959.

Green, Julien. *Journal,* Vols. I and II. Paris: Plon, 1961, 1969.

Greene, Graham. "An Open Letter to Cardinal Archbishop of Paris," translated by Philip Stratford, from *Le Figaro Littéraire,* August 7, 1954. Reprinted in *The Portable Graham Greene.* New York: Viking Press, 1973.

Hell, Henri. *Francis Poulenc.* Paris: Plon, 1958.

Hériat, Philippe. *Retour sur mes pas.* Namur, Belgium: Wesmael-Charlier, 1959.

Jacob, Max, and Claude Valence. *Miroir d'astrologie.* Paris: Gallimard, 1949.

Jammes, Francis. Preface to Colette's *Sept dialogues de bêtes.* Paris: Mercure de France, 1905.

Jouhandeau, Marcel. *Carnets de l'écrivain.* Paris: Gallimard, 1957.

———. *La malmaison.* Paris: Gallimard, 1965.

———. *Que la vie est une fête.* Paris: Gallimard, 1966.

Jouvenel, Bertrand de. "Colette," *Time and Tide,* August 14, 1954.

la Hire, Jean de. *Willy et Colette.* Paris: Adolph D'Espie, 1905.

Lalou, René. *Histoire de la littérature française contemporaine.* Paris: Presses Universitaires de France, 1947.

Lambert, Jean. *Gide familier.* Paris: Julliard, 1958.

Larnac, Jean. *Colette.* Paris: Simon Krâ, 1927.

Léautaud, Paul. *Journal littéraire.* Paris: Mercure de France, 1968.

Lefèvre, Frédéric. "An Hour with Colette," *Living Age,* February 1935.

Maugham, Somerset. *The Summing Up.* New York: Doubleday, Doran and Co., 1938.

Maulnier, Thierry. *Introduction à Colette.* Paris: La Palme, 1954.

Mauriac, Claude. *Conversations avec André Gide*. Paris: Albin Michel, 1951.
(*Conversations with André Gide*. New York: Braziller, 1965.)

Mondor, Henri. *Propos familiers de Paul Valéry*. Paris: Grasset, 1957.

Moreno, Marguerite. *Souvenirs de ma vie*. Paris: Editions de Flore, 1948.

Peyrefitte, Roger. *L'exilé de Capri*. Paris: Flammarion, 1962.

Poulenc, Francis. *Entretiens avec Claude Rostand*. Paris: Julliard, 1954.

Renard, Jules. *Lettres inédites, 1838–1910*. Paris: Gallimard, 1957.

———. *Journal*. Paris: Gallimard, 1965.

Rilke, Rainer Maria. *Letters to Princess Marie Von Thurn und Taxis,* translated by Nora Wydenbruck. New York: New Directions, 1958.

Simenon, Georges. *Portraits souvenirs: Entretiens avec Roger Stéphane*. Paris: RTF et Librairie Jules Tallendier, 1963.

Sondaz, Marie Louise. *Tous les signes expliqués*. Paris: Laffont, 1950.

Virmaux, Alain and Odette. *Colette au cinéma*. Paris: Flammarion, 1975.

Wescott, Glenway. *Images of Truth*. New York: Harper and Row, 1962.

Wilson, Edmund. *The Shores of Light*. New York: Farrar, Straus and Young, 1952.

COLETTE IN ENGLISH

The Blue Lantern [*Le fanal bleu*]

Break of Day [*La naissance du jour*]

The Cat [*La Chatte*]

Chéri and *The Last of Chéri* [*Chéri; La fin de Chéri*]

The Complete Claudine [*Claudine à l'école; Claudine à Paris; Claudine en ménage; Claudine s'en va*]

Creatures Great and Small [*Douze dialogues de bêtes; Autres bêtes; La paix chez les bêtes*]

Duo [*Duo; Le toutounier*]

Earthly Paradise: Colette's Autobiography, drawn from the writings of her lifetime, by Robert Phelps

The Evening Star [*L'étoile vesper*]

Gigi/Julie de Carneilhan/Chance Acquaintances [*Gigi; Julie de Carneilhan; Chambre d'hôtel*]

The Innocent Libertine [*L'ingénue libertine*]

Journey for Myself [*Le voyage égoïste*]

Looking Backwards [selections from *Journal à rebours, Paris de ma fenêtre*]

Mitsou and *Music-Hall Sidelights* [*Mitsou; L'envers du music-hall*]

My Apprenticeships [*Mes apprentissages*]

My Mother's House and *Sido* [*La maison de Claudine; Sido*]

The Other One [*La seconde*]

The Other Woman [selections from *La femme cachée, Paysages et portraits*]

Places [selections from *Trois . . . six . . . neuf, En pays connu, Prisons et paradis, Paysages et portraits, Journal intermittent*]

The Pure and the Impure [*Ces Plaisirs . . .*]

Retreat from Love [*La retraite sentimentale*]

The Ripening Seed [*Le blé en herbe*]

The Shackle [*L'entrave*]

The Tender Shoot and Other Stories [selections from *Bella-vista, Chambre d'hôtel, Le képi, Gigi*]

The Thousand and One Mornings [*Contes des milles et un matins*]

The Vagabond [*La vagabonde*]

I owe my first and eager thanks to Madame Colette de Jouvenel —Bel-Gazou—not only for her generous provision of photographs, documents, and information known only to herself, but for her overall consent to a project which enabled me to immerse myself for several months of 1977 in her mother's world.

Since most of the pictures were collected by myself and friends from old magazines—*Paris-Match, L'Illustration, Annales, Marie-Claire, Figaro Littéraire, Arts,* etc.—and pasted into scrapbooks over at least two decades, I can think of no way to identify the sources and properly credit them. But I would like to record my blanket gratitude for their use here, *ad gloriam* Colette, and to acknowledge the following: Cecil Beaton (pages 246 and 249); Robert Doisneau (page 267); George Platt Lynes and Bernard Perlin (page 208); Lee Miller (page 251); Ned Rorem (page 237, from *Hommages à Marie-Blanche, Comtesse de Polignac,* Jaspard, Polus et Cie, 1965); and David Scherman (page 246).

Finally, I am grateful to three truly guardian angels, Nancy Meiselas, Carmen Gomezplata, and Cynthia Krupat, for the loving care with which they have helped metamorphose a massive clutter of glossy prints and typescript into so tidy an *homage* to the lady who once promised us that "orderliness cures everything . . . *la règle guerit de tout.*"

R. P.